Rebecca Lloyd first started writing when working in Africa as a medical parasitologist. She now runs creative writing courses in Bristol and has had numerous short stories published, winning the inaugural Bristol Short Story Prize 2008 with her story, *The River*. *Halfling* is her first children's novel.

HALFLING

Rebecca Lloyd

WALKER
BOOKS

First published 2011 by Walker Books Ltd
87 Vauxhall Walk, London SE11 5HJ

2 4 6 8 10 9 7 5 3 1

Text © 2011 Rebecca Lloyd

Cover Photograph © 2011 by Michael Prince / photolibrary.com

This book has been typeset in Usherwood

Printed and bound in Great Britain by Clays Ltd, St Ives plc

British Library Cataloguing in Publication Data:
a catalogue record for this book is
available from the British Library

ISBN 978-1-4063-2729-8

www.walker.co.uk

For my lovely daughters,
Emma and Silkie, and their dad.

CONTENTS

Chapter One

Dad had an accident in our car two years ago, and after it happened, he was in a wheelchair. He could do some things for himself, but not everything. Usually, I had to make our dinner when I got home from school, unless Mrs Martin from next door brought us a pie or something.

The hospital said he would be able to walk again, but they didn't know when. He was supposed to do standing-up exercises every day to make his legs stronger, but sometimes he couldn't be bothered and then I had to shout at him. He forgot to take his pills as well if I didn't remind him. "It's for your own good," I kept telling him.

"I know, Danny," he said, "but it feels like I'm going to be in this wheelchair for ever."

One of my jobs was to keep a record of how long he stood up for and how many steps he took. He had to hold onto things, but he could walk a bit if he tried. Last year he could stand and walk for about ten minutes. This year he was up for twenty minutes one day before he got tired.

"Fantastic, Dad," I said. "Twenty minutes this time."

He grinned, but his face looked very white and he had to lie down quickly.

I wasn't in the car when Dad had the accident, but Mum was. They were only going out shopping. Another car crashed into theirs. I didn't know everything about it and Dad didn't tell me much. He just said the same thing if I asked him: "What's done is done, Danny. We just have to get on with things."

It was hard to get on with things, I felt tired all the time and sad. But the people in Cotton Street where we live dropped round to see if we were all right. Sometimes they brought shopping, or flowers. I liked it when we got food from Mrs Martin, because then I didn't have to cook. I didn't mind cooking, but I couldn't make all that many things. Beans on toast, cheese on toast, egg on toast and baked potatoes with coleslaw were what I did best.

Not everybody at my school knew about the accident. Mrs Brown from the library didn't. I went there once to find a cookbook. "You should be reading adventure books, not cookbooks, Danny," she said.

"Yes, but I have to learn some recipes," I told her.

"Doesn't your mum have recipe books?" she asked.

"There's one she made up herself, but I can't read her handwriting."

"Well, she can teach you to cook, surely?"

I didn't know what to say. When I tell people Mum died, they go quiet and flustered and I get embarrassed, but there's no point in *not* saying it. "My mum died in an accident. There's just me and Dad now, and his legs got crushed, so I have to do the cooking," I told her quickly.

"Oh, Danny! I didn't know that," Mrs Brown said, "and I should have known. I apologize." She went red and bit her lip. She was OK. She was shocked, but she didn't ask a lot of questions, or say "you poor little boy" like some people do.

There was a woman who helped us in the house. She came in three times a week and tidied everything up. Dad was always pleased to see her because he didn't like the house to be messy. That was one thing about my dad that was really annoying; he liked everything to be in the right place all the time. It used to drive Mum crazy. She used to say a house has to look a bit lived in. Dad used to say our house looked like a bomb had hit it.

I missed Mum all the time. I tried not to think about her. But sometimes at night she just came into my mind, and wouldn't go away even if I tried to make her. Dad always knew if I'd been thinking about her, and then he made a special effort to do his exercises.

I stayed with Auntie May in London when he was in hospital. I didn't like it there because it was too far away from Cotton Street and I kept worrying about Dad.

"Life at home will be very different when you get back, Danny," Auntie May said. "You're going to have to do a lot of things that adults do, and sometimes it won't seem fair at all."

She was right about that. I had to help Dad get washed in the morning, make his breakfast and tidy things up a bit before I went to school. When I came home again, I had to make our dinner and wash up. It was the same every single day. He could go outside in his wheelchair; we had a ramp at the front door. At the weekend, we sometimes went over to the park, and Dad had special gloves so he could push the wheels round without getting blisters on his hands.

We've always lived in Cotton Street and we know everybody else who lives here. My teacher, Miss Archer, says the people in Cotton Street are a community. That means they try to help each other. Not everybody is nice, though. There's a man at the end of the street who shouts a lot and lives alone. His front door is all bent and the paint is peeling off, but at Easter last year, he put some plastic daffodils in his front window and Dad said he was making an effort.

There's Mrs Malroony as well. She's very old and she stands in the street in her dressing gown and slippers and says hello to everyone. She's funny. She says "love you" or "bless you", even to people she doesn't know, and when she kisses you, you can still feel it on your face no matter how hard you rub it off later.

Most of the people in Cotton Street are old. Mr and Mrs Martin next door are old. They're nice, though, and they've helped me and Dad a lot since the accident. Mr Martin is the churchwarden and he always wears black, and it was Mr Martin's son who made the ramp for us.

Yet it's because of Mr and Mrs Martin that I got confused about what a community is. They talked about other people on the street and didn't always say nice things. When I was there, they tried not to say anybody's name, but I could always guess who they were talking about. They said Mrs Malroony is a bit loopy and that her house is filthy. She lives in the kitchen mostly and doesn't own a single pair of curtains. They said the man who shouts keeps old tyres in his back garden and it was a shame for the people who live next door to him.

When they talked about Mr Seeping, who is three doors down from us, they always whispered. They said nobody had been inside Mr Seeping's house for a long time. I used to see him in the corner shop on Saturdays. One time when I was in there, he came in behind me and patted me on the head – like grown-ups do sometimes. "How is your father now, Daniel?" he asked.

People round here often asked about Dad and I always said the same thing because it was easier. "He's fine," I said.

"Your dad and me used to be good friends when your mum was alive. If you ever need any help with anything, just come and ask me, won't you?"

"Yes, Mr Seeping. Thank you."

I asked Dad about him when I got home. "Mr Seeping said he used to be your friend." Dad looked up quickly and frowned. "He was in the shop just now," I said.

"What else did he say, Danny?"

"I don't know. Nothing. That if I needed anything I could go to him."

"There are lots of people on Cotton Street you can go to, Danny."

I shrugged. "What's wrong with Mr Seeping?"

Dad didn't say anything for a while; he just stared

at the TV. Then he turned round and looked at me. "Nothing," he said.

"He said he was your friend when Mum was alive."

"Did he talk to you about Mum, Danny?"

"No. I just told you what he said."

Dad sighed. "John Seeping and I used to play chess together sometimes, that's all."

"Aren't you friends any more?"

"Life moves on, things change."

That wasn't an answer, and Dad knew it. "Miss Archer told us we were supposed to talk to each other if we're a community," I said. "I think Mr Seeping looks interesting, with all his different hats and things." That wasn't really the truth; it was Mrs Seeping who I thought was interesting. She used to be my friend when she lived in Cotton Street.

"Well, there are a lot of interesting people around here," Dad said. "There's Mrs Malroony for one."

"Why is she so strange, though, Dad? Why does she walk up and down Cotton Street all the time in that old mauve dressing gown?"

Dad looked happy again. "She's very old, Danny. Old people can get a bit strange sometimes; their brains get slightly worn out."

"It's horrible when she tries to kiss me," I said.

Dad laughed. "I know. She eats biscuits a lot and she's always got crumbs on her face."

"Why don't you play chess with Mr Seeping any more? Was he better at it than you?"

Dad looked cross suddenly. "I don't want to discuss John Seeping right now. Just be polite to him, all right?"

"I think about Mrs Seeping sometimes. Do you think she's OK, Dad?"

"Can you still remember her?"

"Of course I can. She used to tell me brilliant stories, and I felt like I was right inside the story. I can't explain it."

"Mrs Seeping never really grew up. I expect you liked her because she was just like a child."

"When she was still here, Mr Seeping had a great big blue car, didn't he?"

"Let's talk about something else," Dad said suddenly. "How's school these days?"

"We're doing a project in community studies, and Miss Archer says we should be kind to everybody, and talk to them properly. You can't just pick and choose," I told him, "and Mr Seeping is part of the community after all."

Dad nodded. "Well, just do as I say, and don't get into a long conversation with John Seeping."

That made me cross; I thought Dad had given up saying "just do as I say". "OK, Dad. I'll do what you say, if you do what I say."

That made him laugh again and he reached over the back of the sofa and squeezed my hand.

The last time I'd seen Mrs Seeping was four years ago, when I was seven. I was on the railway bridge waiting for the fast train to come through. A lot of boys I knew waited for the fast train. It went so fast that it shook the bridge and you could feel it in your feet. It was great.

Mrs Seeping came onto the bridge with some plastic bags and a pink suitcase. "Hello, my friend Danny," she said.

"Hello, Mrs Seeping. Are you going on a train?" I asked her.

She looked up into the sky and her chin was trembling a bit. I liked Mrs Seeping because she was so small, she wasn't much taller than I was, and it's true that it wasn't like talking to an adult.

"I'm going to the seaside, Danny," she said, and she started to cry. I didn't know what to do. I was a bit shocked.

"Don't you like the seaside, Mrs Seeping?"

"I love the seaside. I love it so much that I've decided not to live in Cotton Street any more."

"Does that mean you're going to sell your house?"

She shook her head. "John will still be there at number seven," she said.

"Aren't you going to live with him any more?"

She was still crying. "No. I'm going to live by myself now. I'm going back where I should be."

"Mr Seeping will be sad," I said. I could feel a lump in my throat.

"I know, Danny. I hope you'll be especially kind to him, because he'll be all alone."

Mrs Seeping was funny looking; she always had grey circles under her eyes. She looked as if she was wearing glasses when she wasn't. Her eyes were very round and she blinked a lot.

"But why, Mrs Seeping, why do you have to leave?"

"I used to live in the sea a long time ago, and I miss it terribly."

She was talking so quietly that I had to lean towards her. "Was that when you were a little girl?" I asked.

"I have to go now, dear one, or I'll miss my train."

"I don't want you to go, Mrs Seeping. Please don't go. No one I know says the kind of things you do – about the sea and everything."

She used to talk about different creatures that lived in the ocean, and the things they did. The story I liked best was about the moray eel, and how grumpy and ugly it was.

"I won't forget you," she said, and she kissed me on my forehead.

When she went, I watched her from the bridge

for a while until the train came into the station. I was puzzled. Dad says I sometimes get the wrong end of the stick, which is when you've got the wrong idea. When I was five or something, I thought Dad told me that his grandfather had his arm cut off in the wall. For a long time I wouldn't go near our back wall. "The *war*, darling Danny, not the wall," he said later, and he laughed a lot. I thought Mrs Seeping must have meant she used to live at the seaside, maybe in one of those big houses with a wooden balcony facing the sea.

I liked community studies with Miss Archer because it's about real life and real people. We talked about different people and their jobs. We learnt who was responsible for things, and who you have to talk to if something goes wrong. For instance, it's the council who has to get rid of graffiti on walls, not policemen. If there wasn't a doctor, we wouldn't know what to do when we get sick, and if there wasn't a postman, we wouldn't get any letters. Dustmen are very important too, because without them our streets would be full of rubbish and it would start to smell very quickly and make everybody cross all the time.

When I talked to Dad about people in the community, he told me that everybody who came to help when he and Mum had the accident were very important people. He said ambulance men were the most important people at first, and then at Mum's funeral, the vicar was the most important person, except for Mum herself.

"Later," Dad said, "the surgeon who operated on me was the most important person in my life for a while, except for you of course."

"Now it's the lady who comes to help us, isn't it?" I asked.

"Yes. She's from the council."

"She said I might be able to go on holiday and someone will come and live here while I'm gone and help you."

"Would you like that, Danny?"

I didn't want to say yes in case Dad thought I didn't care about him. "No, I don't want to go anywhere without you."

"I'd be all right if you do want to go," Dad said. "I'll be just fine."

I felt like crying because I did want to go, really. The help lady said there was a big house in the country where I'd meet lots of kids just like me. I was a young carer, she told me. I didn't know it had a name. I thought it was just helping Dad. That's when I wondered if young carers were important people in the community too. She said they were, and I decided to ask Miss Archer more about it the next day.

"Honestly," Dad said, "I'll be all right if you do want to go."

"I can't go and leave you, Dad."

"Yes you can, love. I'll be fine."

I didn't want to talk about it any more. "You have to take your pills. It's eight o'clock," I told him.

He laughed. "What would I do without you?" he said. "How long did I stand up for this evening?"

I looked in my notebook. "Eighteen and a half minutes. Yesterday you walked fifteen steps round the kitchen, but tonight you only walked ten. You have to try harder, Dad."

"I will. I promise. Before you go upstairs, would you just tidy up those magazines? Put them one on top of the other neatly."

I rolled my eyes, but Dad didn't see me do it. I suppose it just made him annoyed when things were out of place and he couldn't do anything about it. I lined all the edges of the magazines up and said good night to him.

Chapter Two

I burnt Dad's toast the next morning and when I tried to make him another piece, he said I'd be late for school, and not to worry. I did worry, though, because it meant he'd be hungry until the help lady came to give him his lunch. I felt stupid and angry.

When I got to school, I saw my teacher getting out of her car. "What's a young carer, Miss Archer?"

"Well, you are, Danny. You and hundreds of other children who have to look after someone in their family."

"Are there a lot of us?"

"I think so."

"Is there anyone else in school who's a young carer?"

She frowned. "Not at the moment, Danny. Why don't you go to the library at lunchtime and see if you can find out more about it?"

All morning I didn't listen to anything in class. I kept thinking about young carers. When lunchtime came, I went to the library. Mrs Brown was there. When I asked her for a book on young carers, she shook her head. "No books, but let's see if we can find anything on the computer," she said. "Come and sit beside me."

There was so much to look at she didn't know where to start. She chose one site and we looked at that. It told you what to do in emergencies. It said it was OK to feel angry sometimes if you were a young carer.

I found out that some young carers had to look after all their brothers and sisters. I felt sorry for them. Some of them had a parent who was never going to get better. It made me very sad. I only had to do things for my dad, and he was just one person. One day he was going to walk again and then everything would be back to normal. I decided I wasn't going to feel angry any more when he asked me to tidy up things that were already tidy.

Mrs Brown put her hand on my shoulder. "Do you have to do everything for your dad at home, Danny?"

"Well, not everything. I help him wash. I have to wash his feet because he can't reach them. Our help lady washes his hair though."

"What else do you do?"

"Make breakfast, cook dinner, unless Mrs Martin

has made us something, and do all the washing-up."

"Which job do you hate most?" she asked.

I didn't exactly mind the jobs, it's just that there wasn't time for anything else at home and that's what I hated. "Tidying up," I told her.

"I hate tidying up too," she said, and that made me laugh.

"Really? But you're a grown-up; all grown-ups do tidying."

"Yes, but it's boring, isn't it, don't you think?"

I laughed again. "Dad wants me to tidy up things that aren't even untidy."

Mrs Brown smiled. "Washing-up, I hate that as well," she said.

"I hate it too," I said. "It makes my arms go itchy. Do you think everybody hates it?"

She shrugged. "Maybe. But the trick is to think about something else while you're doing it."

"What do you think about when you're doing it?" I asked.

She didn't speak for a moment, and then she said, "Mr Brown."

I frowned. "Does he ever do the washing-up?"

She sighed. "Mr Brown lives in his own house now. So, I expect he has his own washing-up to do."

"Does he think about you when he does the washing-up?"

"I don't know, Danny. I like to think so."

I didn't know what to say. I thought of Mrs Seeping on the railway bridge four years ago. I hoped she was happy at the seaside. Then I remembered that she'd asked me to be kind to Mr Seeping. But Dad had told me not to get into a big conversation with him.

In the afternoon, we had biology with Mr Lovemore and that was always funny, so I stopped thinking about young carers. Sometimes Mr Lovemore stands on his desk and nobody is supposed to do that.

He was telling us about toads. He said they were different from frogs. Frogs hop and toads walk. Frogs lay their eggs in a big lump of jelly, but toads' eggs are laid in a long line.

Mr Lovemore climbed onto his desk and everyone cheered and clapped. "The eggs of a toad look like two strings of black pearls. They are so beautiful that you want to give them to your girlfriend to wear as a necklace."

"My mother wouldn't like that," somebody said, "she'd scream."

Suddenly nothing was funny any more. I was thinking about my own mum. I don't think she would have minded a toad-egg necklace at all. I tried to remember her face, but I could only remember her hands and her hair. Her hands smelt of bread and her hair smelt of roses. She had a tiny black mole on her cheek and Dad used to kiss it a lot. But I couldn't remember which cheek it was and that made me panic a bit and my stomach went very tight and my neck went hot.

Mr Lovemore raised his hands in the air to make us quiet. "But, of course, just because you think something in nature is beautiful, you mustn't be tempted to touch it or take it away," he said. "You can look and learn, but you must not touch."

"My dad kills slugs," one of the girls said. "He says you have to, and snails, otherwise they eat all your plants."

Mr Lovemore got off his desk. "Not all slugs eat plants, you know. If you learn how to identify them, you can leave the harmless ones alone."

"Do some people really eat snails?" someone asked.

"They do," Mr Lovemore said. "I've eaten them myself and they are delicious."

That made me feel sick. I started to think about what to cook for dinner. We had some eggs and bacon, but no bread. Mr Khan's shop on the corner would still be open when I got home. But I hoped that Mrs Martin would come over with one of her shepherd's pies. I was thinking I'd ask her about being in a community. Miss Archer had given us a project to do on our community and I didn't know how to start it.

"My dad says that slugs are just snails that have had their shells confiscated for doing something bad," a boy at the back called out.

Mr Lovemore grinned. "Do you believe that, Patrick?"

"I don't know. Maybe."

"And who does the confiscating?"

"Dad never told me, but I think it must be God."

"I expect it's your dad's way of warning you about doing bad things yourself, isn't it?"

"That's what I thought," he said, "only I wasn't sure."

"I don't think you're that gullible, are you, Patrick?"

"Pardon, Mr Lovemore?"

"Well, I mean you don't believe *everything* adults tell you, do you?"

"No, Mr Lovemore, and Dad was smiling when he said it, so I think it really was a joke."

"If you eat snails, Mr Lovemore, then you take something away from nature as well," I heard some-one else say.

Mr Lovemore laughed. "Well, you're right, of course. But I mean sometimes when you see something remarkable in nature, you're tempted to touch it, or poke at it. I know I was like that when I was a boy."

It was hard to think of Mr Lovemore as a boy. "What was the worst thing you did, Mr Lovemore?"

"I collected insects in jars so I could study them, and they often died."

"What's bad about that?"

"Well, they died because of me. Butterflies and beetles and things, and then I felt guilty. In the old days people used to kill butterflies on purpose and pin them onto boards. Sometimes they put them in glass boxes and hung them on their walls just like pictures."

"That's cruel."

"It is cruel, but they didn't know any better in those days. But we do now. We know there are some animals and insects that are close to disappearing altogether unless we look after them. You're very quiet today, Danny Broadaxe."

I jumped. I'd been looking out of the window and thinking about Dad. I was wondering what he'd had for lunch, but I knew it would only be sandwiches. "Sorry, Mr Lovemore."

"Being quiet is nothing to be sorry about, Danny, but not taking part in the class is."

Everything went silent. I went red. "I was listening," I said.

"Listening is good too. But we want to hear what you have to say."

I didn't know what to say for a minute. "Do insects have communities like humans do?" I asked.

Mr Lovemore nodded and smiled at me. "Good

question. Honeybees and ants live in communities, and so do termites. They do different jobs to help their community."

"Are there policemen termites?" someone asked, and we all laughed because that was silly. I tried to think of termites wearing police hats.

"Another good question," Mr Lovemore said. "In fact, some termites are soldiers who look after the worker termites while they build the nest. They're completely different from the workers; they've got great big jaws and they look very dangerous. What's more, they're just as good at walking backwards as they are at walking forward."

"In community studies, we have to do a project about our neighbours," someone said, "and then ask them questions about their life in the community."

Even though I liked Mr Lovemore because you never knew what he was going to say next, I started to look out the window again. I was thinking about how Mrs Seeping used to stand at her front gate and look up and down Cotton Street when I was little. She always called me over to her if she saw me. She never asked me what had happened in school that day like other people did, and I was glad because it was too difficult to decide which bit to say first.

She called me Danny Sea-eyes because I have green eyes, and she only wanted to know about the most exciting thing I'd done that day. I think I must have done a lot of exciting things when I was seven, because I always had something to tell her.

When I got home from school, I could still smell burnt toast in the kitchen. Dad was lying on the sofa looking upset. "What's wrong?" I asked him.

"The help lady didn't show up. Someone else came instead and banged around a lot in the kitchen."

"What did you get for lunch?"

"The usual. Sandwiches. I bet the kitchen's untidy. Go and have a look please, love."

"We're out of bread, Dad. I have to go to Mr Khan's; it'll only take a minute."

"Yes, but tidy the kitchen first; would you?"

I went and checked. There was a teaspoon and a saucer in the sink, nothing else. I washed them up and put them away. I was thinking about our community project again. I'd decided definitely to choose Mrs Martin for my project because she'd lived on Cotton Street since she was a girl and I thought she'd be able to tell me what it was like in the olden days.

Dad called me. "Was everything OK?" he asked.

"Except for a saucer and a teaspoon it was," I told him, "and that *really* doesn't matter much."

Dad sighed. "Let's hope the normal help lady is back on Monday, eh?"

"Yes, Dad. I've got to get bread now."

I wanted to go to the park really. Some people had started to fly kites there. Two boys from my class had asked me to go with them to watch the kites that afternoon, and I'd had to tell them I couldn't. I like kites a lot. I didn't think it would be all that difficult to make one if there was somebody who could help you. But like Dad kept saying, we just had to get on with things.

Mr Seeping was in the shop again. He was ahead of me in the queue, and it was a long one, so it was going to be ages before I'd get served. I thought about going home, but then we'd have no bread for breakfast. Also, I was going to buy sausages for our dinner to cheer Dad up. I'd never cooked them before, but I didn't think it would be too hard.

This time, Mr Seeping had an old black hat on with a small feather in the side of it, not his white knitted one that I liked. He bought two kinds of toffee and a box of matches. Then, when I turned down Cotton Street, he was right there, sitting on Mrs Malroony's wall.

I remembered Mrs Seeping again. Just before her train came, she looked up at me and waved her hand, and I waved back from the bridge. "Go and visit Mr Seeping sometimes, Danny Sea-eyes," she shouted up at me.

I'd been in the shop for a long time, so I just wanted to get back to Dad, but Mr Seeping stopped me.

"Well, young Danny Broadaxe," he said, "how are you today?"

I nodded at him, but it seemed rude. You are supposed to say something back when an adult speaks to you. "Very well, thank you," I said.

I started to walk past him, but he stood up and stepped in front of me. "Are you going on holiday this year, Danny?" I shook my head and looked at my shoes. "How are you doing at school?"

"OK," I said. I tried to look down Cotton Street, but all I could see was the front of his shirt. There was a button missing.

"And how is Matthew?"

Matthew is my dad. "He's still fine," I said.

"It must be hard for you," Mr Seeping whispered.

I looked very quickly at his face and didn't know what to say next. So I shrugged and looked away. I wished Mrs Malroony would come out of her house and interrupt us. The funny thing was, she did open her door, but when she saw me talking to Mr Seeping, she stared for a while and then closed the door quietly.

"I have to get home now. I've got to make tea," I told him.

"Life must be tough for you, Danny."

I knew I had to answer even though it wasn't a question; adults expect you to. "Well, you just have to put up with it," I said.

"Mrs Seeping used to like you a lot. Did you know that?"

I shrugged. "I used to like her too."

"You know you can talk to me any time if you feel sad about things, Danny."

"Thank you, Mr Seeping. Dad's waiting for his dinner. He only ever gets sandwiches for lunch and I think they're usually cheese, and I burnt his toast this morning."

I tried to step past him again, but he put his hand on my arm. "Sit here with me for a minute," he said, and I had to; I couldn't just run away from him. It was all very well for Dad to tell me not to get into long conversations with him, but I obviously couldn't just go straight away.

"When I was little, Mrs Seeping was always nice to me," I told him because I didn't know what else to say.

"Mrs Seeping is wonderful," he answered. "Very wonderful indeed."

"Would she have liked a necklace made of toads' eggs, do you think? Mr Lovemore in school was telling us about toads today."

He laughed loudly. "I'm sure she would, but she'd eat them rather than wear them. Gobble them up, I expect," he added.

"She wasn't afraid of creatures or anything, was she? She used to tell me stories about lobsters and crabs and other weird animals that live in the sea and the funny kind of things they do."

"I've heard those stories as well," Mr Seeping said. "Did she tell you about the moray eel?"

"Yes, and how grumpy it is all the time."

I didn't feel so bad any more. I didn't have to tell Dad that I'd had a conversation with Mr Seeping.

"Do you like animals, Danny?"

"Yes, of course."

"Do you have any pets at home?"

"No. Mum wanted a dog, but Dad didn't because of the mess. Dad hates mess. Probably more than most people."

"Do you think your dad is getting any better?" He turned his head and looked into my face, so I looked straight back at him.

"Sometimes I think he is and sometimes I think he isn't. When he falls over, he gets upset and moody. Then if he gets moody, I get moody."

"I am sorry, that must be difficult."

"Yes, but when he does his exercises and stands up for a while, he's OK."

"I expect it's a bit of a relief to go to school every day. It's going to be harder for you when the holidays come."

"I know, but you just have to carry on," I said. I was getting worried now; it seemed as if I'd been with him for ages. "I have to go, Mr Seeping. I've got to cook dinner and start my project."

"What's your project?"

"Doing something for a neighbour and writing about what a community is."

"I have something very special you could do."

"I was thinking of asking Mrs Martin," I said, "because she lived in Cotton Street in the olden days, so she might know some interesting things."

"Look, Danny, I've got to go away next week, and I need someone to feed my fish. Could you do it for me? I'd pay you."

I shook my head. "We're not supposed to take any money," I told him.

"I don't know who else to ask. I don't know any other boys around here, Danny. I'd be so grateful if you'd say yes."

I couldn't see a way out of it. "I'd have to ask Dad," I told him.

"Will you do that, then? I'll be away for six days and you only have to feed them five times. I know Mrs Seeping would be really pleased to think of you looking after the fish."

"I don't know if Dad would let me," I said. "Besides, I'd have to ask you questions as well for my project."

"What kind of questions?"

"About your life in Cotton Street."

"My life in Cotton Street," he said slowly. He didn't speak again for a minute; he looked as if he was thinking very hard. "I suppose that's fair, Danny. Will you ask your dad if it's OK?"

I nodded, and he smiled as I got up to leave.

Dad was in his wheelchair when I got home. He didn't ask me why I'd been so long. Maybe I hadn't been so long. It just seemed that way. I decided not to ask him about Mr Seeping's fish until he looked as if he was in a good mood.

The trouble with sausages is that when you try to turn them over, they won't always go. It would be much better if they were square instead of round. Ours were a bit burnt on one side, and a bit pink on the other. Dad was hungry; he ate fast. I didn't feel hungry at all. I was worried. I was going to have to ask him about Mr Seeping's fish quite soon. When eight o'clock came, Dad took his pills without being reminded for once.

"Walking practice," I said.

Dad pulled himself out of his wheelchair and held onto the edge of the sofa. He had to go around it only holding on with one hand.

I looked at the clock. "Start now and go slowly," I told him.

He had to concentrate hard, but this time he wasn't shaking. He watched his feet while he did it.

"How's that?" he asked when he'd been round three times.

"You're doing really well, Dad. Twice more, and then you have to go the other way using the other hand."

He looked a bit flushed. "It's not easy, Danny. Are you timing me?" he asked.

"Yes, of course I am. You've been on your feet for twelve minutes. I want you to get up to twenty-two minutes if you can."

He laughed a little bit. "You're very hard on me."

"I know, Dad, but you have to do it. It's hard on me too. I feel really bad sometimes when I see you trying to walk."

He had to stop after nineteen minutes. He looked tired and shaky. When he was lying on the sofa again, he reached for my hand and squeezed it. "You know you can take that holiday you were talking about, don't you, my love?"

I nodded and looked away. "I don't want to talk about it right now. I've got to work on my project, and that's all I'm thinking about."

"Look, Danny, I feel so rotten about you sometimes. All the work you do. You shouldn't have to at your age. I want to do something to make it better for you. Is there anything you can think of?"

"There's one thing, but I don't think you'll agree."

"Try me."

"I know you'll say no."

"Oh, come on, love. What?"

"For my project, I have to do something for someone in our community." I held my breath.

"Go on."

I couldn't go on. He looked grey and worn out. I couldn't tell him then. "I'll speak to you about it in the morning," I said.

"OK, Danny. And don't look so serious. I'll do anything I can to make things better for you."

Chapter Three

I sometimes thought I shouldn't push Dad so hard about walking. He didn't really seem to be improving. But even worse than that, I shouldn't have said anything to him about Mr Seeping before I went to school. We had a big row and I slammed the door on my way out.

"I've decided to choose Mr Seeping for my project," I'd told him.

"No you haven't," Dad said quietly. He was smiling at me. "Good joke."

"I'm going to feed his fish while he's away next week."

Dad shook his head. "Choose someone else. What about Mrs Malroony?"

"I don't want to do Mrs Malroony because she sometimes talks nonsense and she doesn't listen to what you say back. What's wrong with Mr Seeping, anyway?"

Dad looked away. I stared at the tablecloth. I really

wanted to know. "I'll tell you sometime, but not now, Danny. Just do as I say and please choose a different neighbour."

"If Mrs Seeping had still been here, would you have let me then?"

"Vaquita Seeping," Dad said, "that funny little soul. Let's not talk about it right now; you'll be late for school."

"I don't care!" I shouted. "You can't just say no and not tell me why."

"Yes I can. I'm your father, or had you forgotten that?"

"How could I forget it? I have to look after you. I have to cook and clean and tidy things up that don't even need it." I stood up quickly and picked up my school bag. "You just think things are in a mess all the time when they're not."

Dad clenched his fists and lowered his head so I couldn't see his face. He was shaking. He stood up slowly, and gripped the edge of the table. "You're eleven years old, Danny, you do what I say!"

I left the house quickly and didn't even wait to see if he could get into his wheelchair again. I didn't care. On the way to school, I felt miserable. Now I'd have to tell Mr Seeping I wasn't allowed to look after his fish, and it was all Dad's fault. I wanted Mum badly. I almost didn't go to school that day, I just wanted to keep walking and never stop, and not have to speak to another adult ever again. They didn't understand anything.

We had community studies in the morning; we were talking about caring for people. I didn't listen. I looked out of the window most of the time. I was feeling really bad about Dad. I was worried that he'd fallen over after I'd left the house, and that maybe he couldn't get up again, and he was lying on the kitchen floor.

I felt angry with Mr Seeping for asking me to feed his fish and getting me into trouble in the first place. I started to cry a couple of times in class and had to duck my head and swallow a lot so nobody saw me.

I was glad when it was lunchtime. I went straight to the playground and sat on the seat by the school pond. Then Mr Lovemore came over. He was wearing his yellow jumper with holes in it.

"Hello, Danny boy," he said.

"'Lo, Mr Lovemore."

"Do you want to help me look for water-snail eggs?" he asked.

"I suppose so," I said, looking over his shoulder.

"What's wrong?"

"Nothing much. Just fed up with everything."

"You do look upset. Has someone been bullying you?"

I shook my head. There used to be a boy who

called me Blunt-axe and other stupid things because my surname is Broadaxe, but that was ages ago. "I'm fine," I said. I don't think he believed me.

"Well, let's see what we can find in the pond." He picked up a water-lily leaf very carefully and looked on the underneath of it. "See that? Snail eggs, that's what I'm looking for."

I bent down close to the water. On the back of the leaf was something that looked like a piece of see-through toothpaste. I could just see tiny white specks in it. Mr Lovemore tore off the piece of leaf with the eggs on it and put it in a jar of water.

"How did you know it was there?" I asked.

"I was almost certain it would be; water snails like to find a flat surface to lay their eggs on."

"What're you going to do with it, Mr Lovemore?"

"I'm making another pond in my garden at home, and I need to stock it up with animals that live in fresh water. You'd be surprised how quickly these little fellows will grow once they've hatched out. Do you have a pond at home, Danny?"

I shook my head. "I don't think my father would like it, it'd be far too messy, I expect." I felt my throat go tight.

"What a funny idea. There's nothing messy about a pond. It's a wonderful little world all of its own. You can stare into a pond for ages and see all kinds of things. I've got frogs and newts in mine, and in spring-time all the toads gather at the pond and call out to each other. Lovely little mournful cries they've got, you know, quite heartbreaking."

"It wouldn't be any use telling my dad things like that."

"Well, I suppose there are some people who like nature, and other people who don't. You like nature, don't you, Danny?"

"Yes, I do," I said. For a moment, I wondered if I should tell him about the row with Dad, and then I changed my mind. It was too complicated and I didn't really know where to start. "Do you think it's good or bad to feel guilty about things?" I asked him.

"Guilty about things? Oh, definitely good."

"How can it be good when it makes you feel miser-able?" I asked.

Mr Lovemore frowned. "If you feel guilty about something it shows that you care," he answered.

I was thinking that when I got home I'd tell Dad a lie. I'd say I wasn't going to feed Mr Seeping's fish but do it anyway. Dad didn't always know where I went when I was outside, and it wouldn't take all that long to feed some fish. "If you tell a lie you feel guilty, don't you, Mr Lovemore? And then you feel bad."

"Yes, you do," he said.

"Is that the real reason people don't tell lies, so

they don't have to feel bad?"

Mr Lovemore laughed. "Well, maybe, for some people. But it's bad to tell lies because then you're fooling somebody – and that's not caring about them. Have you told a lie to someone, Danny?"

"No. But I've been thinking about it."

"Well, my advice to you is don't do it. Lying always makes things worse. Avoid it if you can. Tell the truth always."

"Even if it causes a row?"

"Yes. Definitely."

"Is it only children who tell lies, Mr Lovemore?"

"Oh, Danny, I only wish it were."

"I thought it was something you grew out of."

He smiled at me. "I don't like seeing you sad. Sometimes in class you're just not with us, are you?"

"I suppose not."

"You know where to find me if you ever want to talk about things, don't you?"

I nodded. A few grown-ups had said that to me, but I didn't think I would speak to anyone because I couldn't see how it would change anything.

When I got home, Mrs Martin had made us spaghetti and meatballs and left the dish in the oven. I was really glad because I didn't feel like cooking at all. The sitting-room door was open and I could see Dad. He was in his wheelchair doing his ankle exercises. I tried to go upstairs without saying anything to him. I didn't want to talk.

"Danny!" he called.

I went to the door, but didn't go in. "What?"

"Sorry."

"Me too. Sorry, Dad."

"I've been thinking about you all day, love."

"I've been thinking about you too," I said. "I've had a horrible day."

"You said John Seeping was going on holiday and you just have to go into his house and feed his fish?"

"Yes. That's all."

"Oh, well, I expect it'll be all right."

"Are you sure?"

"Yes, Danny. You can do it."

"I'll have to go round and tell him it's OK, then."

I thought about what Mr Lovemore had said about lying when we were by the pond. "That's not really all I have to do, though, Dad. When he comes back from holiday, I'm going to have to ask him some questions about his life in Cotton Street."

Dad sighed. "We'll cross that bridge when we come to it," he said very quietly.

I walked into the sitting room then, and stood in front of him so I could see him properly. "That means Mrs Seeping will come into it," I said, "because I'll probably ask him why she went off to live by the sea."

"I don't think that's the kind of question you should be asking, Danny. It's about living in the community, isn't it?"

"Well, Mrs Seeping was in the community too, once," I answered quickly. "Even if no one else remembers her, I do."

"You really liked her, didn't you?"

"She was great, Dad. She never asked silly questions like other grown-ups do."

Dad laughed, and threw a cushion on the floor for me to sit on. "She certainly was strange. One of the strangest people I've ever come across. You talked to her a lot when you were little. You used to wait at her gate to see if she'd come out of the house."

"I know I did. I miss her, not nearly as much as Mum, of course, but I do miss her." I sat down on the cushion and looked at Dad in his wheelchair. "I wish things didn't have to change all the time."

"I know what you mean, love. But there you are; we just have to get on with it, don't we? What did you used to talk to Vaquita Seeping about anyway, can you remember?"

"We used to talk about exciting things, Dad, only it wasn't really like talking. It was like being in a different place, like not being in Cotton Street at all. I can't really explain it properly. She told me she dreamt about the sea, and then I started dreaming about the sea as well – swimming under the water." Dad stared at me and didn't interrupt. "I saw her at the train station when she was leaving. She kept looking back, as if she didn't really want to go away from Cotton Street. She was crying."

"You could have been the last person to see her, Dan. I wish you'd told me. Come up on the sofa with me."

Dad said the women on Cotton Street worried about John Seeping after Vaquita left. They used to look over the fence and notice how he put his washing on the line. If he hung it out in a careless way, they knew he was feeling bad. But if all the socks were together and the tea towels were next to each other and everything was neat, they thought he was a bit happier.

Not everybody in Cotton Street looks after their front gardens. Mr and Mrs Martin, who have yellow and pink roses in theirs, were always saying people should take care of their gardens. Mrs Malroony's has a few weeds in it, the man who shouts has old rusty bicycles in his and Mr Seeping's front garden is covered in long grass that must have been a lawn once.

When I got to number seven, I stood at the front gate for a while and looked at Mr Seeping's house. His front-room curtains were closed. I walked up the path, slowly. There was a doorbell, but it was rusty and it didn't work. There was a fish on the doorstep made of stone.

I knocked on the door and waited. Nobody came and I couldn't hear anything. I knocked louder, but only three times because I didn't want him to think I was rude. He still didn't come.

I turned back towards the gate and thought of going home. Then I decided to look through the letter box. I couldn't see anything much, just dark shapes everywhere. Then suddenly the door opened just a little bit, and one of Mr Seeping's eyes was looking at me. I could hear a funny noise in the house behind him, a strange wailing sound, but very soft.

"Dad says I can feed your fish next week, Mr Seeping."

"Oh, good. I was getting worried about them. I can't talk now. I'll meet you on Saturday in that café on Merchant Street at eleven o'clock and give you your instructions."

When I got home and told Dad I had to meet Mr Seeping in the café, he sighed. "Look, Danny, just because you said you'd feed his fish, you don't have to if you don't want to."

"I do want to. He said he'd give me some money which means he wants me to badly."

"I'd better go with you just to see that everything is all right."

I didn't understand my dad sometimes; I think he got worried about things all the time because of not being able to walk. I couldn't imagine what that was like. "Everything *is* all right, Dad," I said.

"No. I'll go with you. I haven't spoken to John for ages."

It was as if he thought I was just a little kid again. "You can't get into the café in a wheelchair because of the steps."

Dad shrugged. "Well we'll call him outside then. I'm sorry, Danny, but I am going with you, and that's that."

When it was Saturday and we'd had breakfast, Dad and I went to the café together. I could see Mr Seeping inside. I tapped on the window and he came out. When he saw my dad, he went very pale and frowned. "How are things, Matt?" he asked. He didn't even look at me.

"Things are as you see them, John," my dad answered. "How are things with you?"

Mr Seeping laughed, but he sounded nervous. "I walk everywhere now. I don't even own a bike."

"Danny tells me you want him to feed your fish while you're away."

"That's right. I hope it's OK with you, Matt?"

Dad didn't say anything for a while and I felt embarrassed. Mr Seeping was wearing a green bobble hat, and he kept touching it as if he thought it wasn't on properly. Dad folded his arms and shrugged. Then he looked into Mr Seeping's face. "Life's hard for Danny right now," he said, "and he doesn't need to know things that would make it harder still. And that means anything, John, anything at all."

Mr Seeping took a step backwards and looked surprised. "I wouldn't dream of it, Matt."

"So what does he have to do?"

Mr Seeping turned to me. "The key is under the stone trout on my doorstep, Danny. The fish are in the front room, and the fish food is on the little table. Just put a couple of pinches into each tank every day after school. That's all. Don't stay and watch them eat it. You only need to be in the house for a few minutes."

"Have you got a lot of fish, John?" Dad asked.

Mr Seeping touched his hat again. "Yes, there are quite a few tanks, all along one wall."

"Understand what you have to do, Danny?" Dad asked me a bit sharply.

"Of course," I said. "It's easy."

"Just in and out of the house quickly," Mr Seeping said. "You don't have to hang about, OK?"

"OK," I said.

Dad turned his wheelchair around and set off down the road without even saying goodbye to Mr Seeping, and I thought that was rude.

Chapter Four

"Going to number seven," I said to Dad when I got home from school on Monday.

"Is everything tidy in the kitchen?" he asked.

"I've just looked, Dad. It is."

"Don't be long, then."

The key was under the stone trout like Mr Seeping said it would be. His house was just the same as ours, so I knew where the front room was. It felt strange for a minute going inside another person's place when they weren't there. It was quite dark inside and I could hear a tap dripping in the kitchen at the end of the hall.

I opened the front-room door, and was so amazed that I made a loud noise. I thought Mr Seeping would have an ordinary sofa and some armchairs and a TV like we have, but there wasn't anything like that in there.

I pulled the door shut behind me and walked to the middle of the room. It was just like being inside a huge cave under the sea, and it smelt like the sea too, salty and fresh. There were patches of light on the ceiling that changed shape all the time, and everything seemed speckled and soft, and green and blue. I could hear a murmuring noise, but it was so faint that I wasn't certain it was really there. For a while, I couldn't do anything but look around, it was like being in a dream.

There were hundreds and hundreds of fish in eight big square tanks along one of the walls. I could see the fish food on a little table and I know I said I'd just feed them and go, but I wanted to look at them all properly. So I walked from one tank to the next and looked into each one for a long time.

I kept thinking I'd found the most beautiful fish, and then I'd see another one even more beautiful. Down at the bottom of the tanks were some weird ones that seemed to be stuck to the rocks. I didn't even know they were fish until they moved suddenly; they looked just like rocks themselves. There were other creatures in the tanks as well that weren't fish, things that looked like tiny grey lobsters with long feelers and eyes that stuck out on stalks, and really frail legs.

I liked the tiny bright blue fish that swam about together and turned around suddenly at the same time, a bit like starlings do when they fly about in a flock in the evening. I tried to look at all the different fish faces. Some had fat lips that stuck out and others had little round lips that hardly moved. One of them looked like Mrs Brown in the library and I laughed. That was when I heard the strange noise I'd heard the first time I came to the house. It reminded me of when our music teacher makes the tuning fork hum. It was just like that, very high and very lovely, and somehow sad.

I looked behind me and there wasn't anything there. The noise changed then, and it sounded a bit like a bumble-bee trying to get outside again when the window's closed. Then it stopped, and the only sound I could hear was a car on the street outside. I realized I'd been holding my breath, so I breathed out loudly and walked to the table.

I put two pinches of food into each tank. Some of the fish came to the top of the water and ate very quickly and butted into each other. I kept seeing new fish all the time. Some of them looked so fantastic it was hard to believe they were real creatures. I was so interested in them that I shivered.

I wished Dad could see them. I wished Dad could walk. Mum would have loved Mr Seeping's fish; she liked anything in nature, even ordinary brown spiders that other people think are scary.

I don't know how long I stared into the fish tanks,

but I'd been there for much longer than a couple of minutes, and I suddenly got scared that Dad would be worried. I had to think all the time about the different things that might make him worried, and try not to let them happen. That's probably what people meant when they said I had to be like an adult.

I walked out into the hall. Something made me look up the stairs, a shadow or a little movement. I had the idea for a moment that someone else was in the house, but decided it was because I was nervous that Dad would be cross with me when I got home.

Just as I put my hand out to open the door, I thought I heard someone say my name, but I couldn't tell where the voice came from. It startled me, and I could feel my heart beating harder. That happens in school sometimes if I'm daydreaming; living in my own world, as Miss Archer calls it. Someone speaks to you, and for a minute, you don't know who it is or where you are.

I turned round and looked up the stairs. The window on the landing at the top was smaller than ours at home, and it didn't give much light. I waited for a moment and listened. I could hear the tap dripping in the kitchen again, but nothing else. Yet I still had the feeling of not being alone, and it began to frighten me.

"What's the matter?" Dad asked me when I got home again.

"Nothing, everything's fine. Have you done your ankle exercises?"

He nodded, but kept looking at me. "You're as white as a ghost," he said. "Were the fish OK?"

"Yes, of course they were. What do you want for tea?"

"Are they tropical fish?"

I swallowed hard. "I don't really know, Dad. I've never seen anything like them before."

"How many were there?"

"Hundreds and hundreds. What do you want for tea?"

"Fish fingers if we've still got some."

Dad laughed and I frowned at him. It wasn't a very good joke, and I was still thinking about someone calling out my name at number seven.

I waited until we'd finished eating before I said anything else. "You know when you were friends with Mr Seeping?"

"Yes?"

"Well, did you ever go inside his place?"

"No. The Seepings kept themselves to themselves pretty much. I used to meet John at the café on Merchant Street for a game of chess from time to time, but I was never invited to the house. People were very curious about those two. Mrs Seeping very rarely spoke to anyone; she didn't pass the time of day on Cotton Street."

"What does pass the time of day mean, Dad?"

"Oh, stand about in the street and chat to people, you know?"

"That's what Mrs Martin does all the time. She doesn't always say nice things about people, though."

"I know, but she's very kind to us, isn't she? And when Vaquita Seeping left Cotton Street, she used to take pies and stews round to John for a while and leave them on the doorstep."

"No one else lives at number seven except Mr Seeping, do they, Dad?"

"No. He's lived alone since she went."

"Did Mum like Vaquita?"

"Yes, love. She used to call her the strange little rolly person from number seven."

"Do you think Mum would've liked a necklace made of toads' eggs?"

"You say the most peculiar things sometimes. What made you think of that?"

"Mr Lovemore in school was talking about toads. I think he really likes them. He said their calls are heart-breaking. He's building a new pond in his garden. I wish we could have a pond, it's a little world all of its own."

Dad cleared his throat. "Your biology teacher is what you call an eccentric. That means someone who goes their own way and doesn't bother much about what other people think of them."

"Are there a lot of eccentrics, do you think?"

"No, they're rare people, Danny, very rare." Dad yawned and rubbed his forehead.

"You could do your walking practice now," I told him.

"Can it wait a while? I want you to tell me about John Seeping's house."

"No, Dad. It's got to be now, you're already tired. There's nothing to say about the house. It's the same as ours, just ordinary, except for the fish."

I was tired as well, I wanted to go upstairs and be by myself, but I knew that if I let him off walking practice, I'd feel bad about it the next day. There had been a man from the hospital who came to our house sometimes and made Dad do special exercises, but that was only for about six months, and then we had to do everything by ourselves.

Dad yawned again. "I expect they're tropical fish. People say they're quite hard to look after."

"I don't know what they are, but they're beautiful and strange. Can you stand up now, Dad, and start?"

I had to hoover the upstairs landing before I went to school the next day, because Dad was sure it needed doing. It made me a bit late, but I knew it wouldn't matter because our first lesson was biology.

When I walked into the classroom, Mr Lovemore said, "Ah, Danny Broadaxe, good to see you," just as if I was an adult. He was wearing his old yellow jumper again. All the desks and chairs had been pushed to the back of the room and everyone was sitting on the floor. Mr Lovemore was as well. "Why do you think the peppered moth looks almost the same as the tree it lives on?" he asked.

"By accident," someone said.

Mr Lovemore shook his head and looked serious. "There aren't many things you can call an accident in nature," he said. "There's a reason for everything, even if people haven't worked out what it is. Sit there, Danny, and pay attention."

"All moths look the same anyway. They are all brown," one of the boys whispered.

"You need to look harder, if that's what you think," Mr Lovemore answered quickly. "So why *do* you think the peppered moth looks the same as the tree it lives on?" Nobody knew the answer. "What eats moths, do you think?"

"Birds, maybe?" someone said.

Mr Lovemore smiled. "That's right, they do, and they have to find them first, don't they?"

I knew the right answer suddenly. I remembered the fish at the bottom of Mr Seeping's tanks – and how I didn't even know they were fish until they moved. "It would be hard to see a moth properly if it looked the same as the tree," I said. "So it could hide from birds and wouldn't get eaten."

"Well done, Danny! Lots of insects look similar to the places they live in, so that other creatures who want to eat them can't see them easily."

I felt pleased. I could see it now; it was obvious. "But not all insects are like that," I said. "What about wasps? You can see them easily."

"My dad hates wasps," one of the girls said. "He says they could kill you. When he sees one, he gets really scared and flaps his arms about and goes a funny colour. One day there was a wasps' nest in our attic. I saw it and it was huge, and Dad got frightened and ran down the stairs very fast, and my mum had to make him a cup of tea and call the council out."

Everybody laughed; it was hard not to.

"So how do wasps protect themselves from something that wants to eat them?" Mr Lovemore asked us.

"By stinging everything," the boy next to me said.

"That's right. So birds would learn not to eat wasps, don't you think?" People nodded, and Mr Lovemore grinned. "But, does anyone know what a hoverfly is?"

"It's a black and yellow striped kind of a fly," I said, looking at his yellow jumper.

"It is. How does having black and yellow stripes help it?"

We didn't know the answer again. I could hear the clock ticking. It reminded me of the tap dripping in Mr Seeping's house. I should've gone upstairs and had a look around. Maybe there was a burglar there all the time. I suddenly felt a bit sick. I had to go to number seven four more times before Mr Seeping got back from holiday.

Mr Lovemore went to the front of the class and climbed up onto his desk. "Well, it's one of nature's lies," he said. "If hoverflies have black and yellow stripes, they look like wasps, so birds don't eat them. But people don't have to be scared of them because they can't sting."

"But how can you tell the difference between a wasp and a hoverfly?" someone behind me asked.

"You have to learn to look hard," Mr Lovemore answered. "A fly's face is nothing like a wasp's face. Flies have great big bulging eyes, and some of them have quite hairy faces."

The boy who used to bully me said, "I don't want to look at flies' faces. That's just silly."

Mr Lovemore shrugged, and then looked a bit cross. "Then I hope the world isn't just a blur to you, Andrew, as you grow up. You have to look and listen hard to understand the world, you know."

Everyone went quiet as they left the classroom because Mr Lovemore wasn't smiling any more. I waited behind until they'd all gone. "Can I ask you something?"

"Yes, what is it, Danny?"

"Do you know any eccentric people?"

Mr Lovemore frowned and stroked the front of his jumper. "That's not a biology question."

"I know it isn't. But I'm interested. I think I've got an eccentric neighbour. I'm doing my community studies project on him, and I have to ask him questions about his life."

"I'm not the best person to ask. I know about insects and pond life. I don't know as much about people. What makes you say he's eccentric?"

"He's got a room full of fish, and when you go in there, it's like being under the sea. It even smells like the sea, and there's a sound that I think is meant to be waves on a beach."

Mr Lovemore stared at me, and I wondered if he thought I was making it up. "Come out to the pond with me and talk to me there. I'm collecting a few of the big water snails today."

Apparently, there are three kinds of water snails you can usually find in ponds, but the ones in the school pond were called the great pond snail. Instead of having horns with eyes at the end like normal snails, they have triangular things on their heads that look just like cats' ears. Some of the snails in the school pond are huge, and their shells come to a sharp point at the end.

"Is everything OK, lad?" Mr Lovemore asked me. "You were late again today, weren't you?"

"But I was paying attention."

"Yes, you were. You gave some good answers. But you were biting your fingernails and looking out of the window sometimes."

I felt my throat squeeze up. I picked at some grass by the edge of the pond and stared into the water. "Sometimes I wish I was an animal or something, and I was just free," I told him.

"I used to think that when I was a boy as well. I wanted to be an eagle."

"Oh well. I suppose we just have to get on with everything."

"Mrs Brown told me that you asked her if young carers were important people in the community."

"I know. But it's only really grown-ups who are important," I said.

Mr Lovemore shook his head. "Every single one of us is important, Danny."

"Even eccentric people?"

He looked at me with his head on one side. "Even them," he said.

"What kind of fish have you got in your pond at home?"

"Oh, I don't keep fish in any of my ponds," he said. "I like to think of fish swimming freely, not cooped up in a pond and going round and round for ever."

"I feel like I'm going round and round all the time," I told him. "I have to keep cleaning up at home, otherwise Dad gets upset and then he doesn't do his exercises properly. Is your house tidy, Mr Lovemore?"

"Oh, dear me, no. There are so many books on my kitchen table now that I can't eat there any more, and I expect people would consider that rather eccentric. I do think about cleaning up sometimes, but I always find something more interesting to do."

"Are *you* an eccentric, then?"

He laughed and bit his lip. "People do think that about me," he said.

"Do you mind?"

I thought he'd say no, but he didn't. His shoulders dropped and he started picking at the grass, like me. "I do sometimes, a little bit."

"Do you live by yourself?"

"Not exactly. There's my cat, Horrid Boy, but he doesn't say much."

"I wish I had my mum," I said, and my eyes felt hot.

"Things are hard for you at the moment, aren't they?"

"I feel as if I'm alone sometimes, but I'm not

actually because I've got Dad. But I've started noticing that some people really are alone. Mrs Brown in the library doesn't live with Mr Brown any more, you live by yourself, and Mrs Seeping, one of our neighbours who I really, really liked, left home ages ago."

"Well, just remember that life is mysterious, Danny, and you never know what's going to happen next. I think we should all try not to forget that." He chose five large snails and put them in a jar with some water. "Have a look at them, aren't they handsome?"

I liked their faces and their ears a lot; they made me smile, and I felt a bit better. "Yes," I said, "they are handsome."

Chapter Five

Dad was looking happy when I got home. "Guess what I did?" he said.

"What?"

"I stood up without holding onto anything, and then I walked once round the sofa without touching it."

"Honest, Dad, did you really?"

"Well, not very fast, but I did do it. The help lady was here and she watched me. She thought that if I kept at it, I'd be walking properly in no time."

I did feel pleased, but I was worried. I kept thinking about the funny noise I heard at number seven and how it felt as if I wasn't the only person in the house.

"You know when you were a boy, Dad?"

"Yes?"

"Did you ever wish you were an animal instead of a human being?"

Dad laughed. "I don't think so; I don't remember anything like that."

"Mr Lovemore did, he wanted to be an eagle."

"Did he really?"

"You know – when you're feeling miserable and you don't want to be responsible for things any more? And you look at an animal and you wish you were one too."

"Come here, son," Dad said very softly.

"I can't right now, I've got to feed the fish and I want to get it over with."

"You want to get it over with? Is there something wrong?"

"Not particularly."

He stared at me, but he didn't make me sit next to him. "If there was something the matter, you would tell me, wouldn't you?"

"Do you think life is mysterious, Dad?"

He laughed again, and then stopped suddenly. "It certainly is. You can't ever tell what's going to happen." He glanced down at his legs and then looked away quickly. "So if you could be an animal instead of a person, what animal would you be, love?"

"Something in the ocean, I think. Maybe a seal, so I could swim about all the time and eat fish and not have to bother about anything." Dad tried to smile at me, but his eyes looked worried. "I have to go now," I told him. "You could do your ankle exercises."

"Well hurry back. We've got a chicken pie from Mrs Martin and I'm hungry," he said.

When I got to Mr Seeping's house, I tried to open the door without making any noise. I stood in the hallway for a long time and looked up the stairs. Then I realized that the stairs were wet. I started to feel nervous again.

Everything was the same in the front room, except I couldn't help feeling that someone had been in there because the curtains were a little bit open. The fish looked fine, and I decided not to stay and watch them, but to get home to Dad quickly. Mr Seeping had told me not to hang about in the house anyway.

I put two pinches of fish food in the tanks, like the day before. I did stay for one minute to watch them eating because I couldn't help it, they were so funny the way they all crowded together and tried to push each other out of the way. Then I put the lid back on the fish food and turned around.

That was when I realized that there was some-one standing just inside the room. It was very dark; I couldn't see much. My legs went all weak and my heart started beating so hard that I could hear it. I felt as if I was a statue, and then everything went a weird yellow colour for a minute.

"It's my friend Danny, Danny Sea-eyes, isn't it? Don't be afraid, it's only me."

I knew the voice; it was Mrs Seeping!

I took a couple of steps towards her. She was not supposed to be back in Cotton Street. She was wearing a dark grey swimsuit, and she looked very strange. "Is it really you?" I whispered.

"Of course it's me. Are you feeding the fish?"

I nodded. "Mr Seeping asked me to do it."

"I'm so glad he chose you. Don't look so worried. Come here and let me look at you."

When I reached the door, I looked into her face. She was the same only a bit older, and her hair was very short, and I was taller than her now. "How are you, Mrs Seeping?" I asked.

She shrugged and beamed at me. "I'm as you would expect."

"Have you been swimming?"

"Swimming? No, more's the pity."

I didn't know what to do next. I wondered if I should tell Dad when I got home. He wouldn't believe me, though. "Have you been here all this time?"

"Come with me," she said, and I followed her down the hall to the kitchen.

It was much lighter in the kitchen and I could see her better. I wondered if she was cold. It felt strange being slightly taller than she was. I tried not to stare at her, but I couldn't help it. "When did you come back to Cotton Street?" I asked. "Does anyone else know you're here?"

"I only left for a while, a month or so," she said. "I lost my courage about leaving altogether."

"But I saw you at the train station. You said you were going to live by the sea."

She laughed. "I don't think I said that, I think I told you I was going to live *in* the sea. What's been happening to you, Danny? It must be about four years since I last saw you. You've grown so tall and so strong."

I didn't say anything for a moment because so many things had happened since I was seven. One of them was Mum dying, and I didn't know if Mrs Seeping knew or not. So I changed the subject. "Why did Mr Seeping want me to feed his fish if you were here all the time, Mrs Seeping?"

"Call me Vaquita."

"Dad says it's rude to call grown-ups by their first names."

"Well, it is unless you're invited, and I'm inviting you."

"OK. Why did Mr Seeping want me to feed his fish – *Vaquita*?"

"That's better. Well, he's gone on holiday and he didn't want his fish to starve."

"No, but you're here."

"Oh, John never asks me to do anything around the house."

"Nothing at all?"

"Not the slightest thing. He does everything. Besides, I stay upstairs, I hardly ever come down." She pointed upwards. "I live in the bathroom now, you see."

That made me want to laugh. Nobody actually lives in the bathroom. But I could tell she wasn't joking. "All the time?" I asked.

"Mostly, yes. I haven't been downstairs for ages, but I heard you in the house the other day and thought it might be a burglar. So even though I was scared, I crept down the stairs and found you here. I watched you feeding the fish for a while then went back up again. I didn't know if you'd even remember me and I didn't want to frighten you. Then I wanted to see you badly, and called you, but you didn't come. I'm so glad it *is* you; I've missed talking to you a lot."

"I've missed talking to you as well."

"What was the most exciting thing you did today, Danny Sea-eyes?"

I didn't answer, although it made me smile because she always used to ask that. "It must be horrible to live in a bathroom, Vaquita. What do you do all day?"

She shrugged. "I lie around and think about things."

"Does Mr Seeping have to do the tidying up and everything, then?"

"Yes. He doesn't mind."

"Don't you even cook dinner for him?"

"I don't know how to cook."

"Really! Even I can cook, not everything, but quite a few things."

Vaquita laughed. "Mr Seeping cooks for himself, and he doesn't have to cook for me because I prefer raw food."

"I have to cook for my dad almost every night."

"Doesn't your mother ever cook?"

I shook my head. She didn't know about Mum then, and I didn't feel like telling her. "Does Mr Seeping mind you being up in the bathroom all the time?"

"He'd rather I came down; he made the fish room for me, you know, and it took ages to get it just right. I do go in there sometimes, but it makes me sad."

"It's really beautiful. It's supposed to be what it's like under the sea, isn't it?"

"Meant to be, yes."

I was worried that I'd been with her too long, but I kept thinking of different questions, and I didn't want to leave. I looked around the kitchen. "But what do you eat?"

She frowned. "John brings me what I need."

"Do you really truly live in the bathroom?"

"Yes, Danny."

"Don't you ever go outside?"

"Not any more."

I stood up and looked towards the hall. "I think I'd better go now, or Dad will be worried."

"Are you coming back tomorrow?"

"Yes. I have to."

"I'll look forward to seeing you then, Danny Sea-eyes," she said.

I got out of the front door and closed it behind me without banging it. I didn't know what to feel about everything. I felt all kinds of things. I felt sad to think Vaquita lived in the bathroom, but excited too about seeing her again. When I was seven, I didn't think there was anything strange about her at all, I just liked being with her. Now I was very curious about her though, and it was probably because I was older and noticing more things about grown-ups.

I thought about all the people I knew, Mrs Malroony, Mr Lovemore, the man who shouts – everybody – and there was nobody I could think of who was as strange and interesting as Vaquita.

Dad was looking gloomy when I got back home. I went into the kitchen to peel some potatoes to go with the chicken pie. I didn't want him to see my face in case he saw that I was excited. Something was *wrong* at number seven, but I couldn't work out what it was. I supposed that if Mr Seeping was an eccentric, then

Vaquita was as well. People should be able to live how they wanted; Dad told me Mum used to say that. Yet I'd never heard of someone who just lived in a bathroom. It would be so boring.

"What would be boring, love?" Dad asked, and I realized I must have been talking out loud.

"Boring to live in one room all the time."

"Oh, I don't though. I do go out in the wheelchair sometimes when you're at school. Perhaps not as often as I should, but I do go. Don't worry about me."

"I didn't mean you, Dad."

I was dying to tell Dad about Vaquita straight away, but it was all so strange that I wanted to think about it for a while by myself. Anyhow, I knew that it was best for Dad if his life was calm and ordinary and the same things happened all the time. I thought I'd wait until Mr Seeping got home before I said anything, since it was only four more days. Although, maybe Mr Lovemore would be able to explain it since he was an eccentric himself and wouldn't get cross with me, or worried like Dad might.

When I was little, I used to tell Mum and Dad everything, but tons of things changed after Mum died. Mrs Brown said that young carers lose a lot of their childhood. She said they have to grow up far too fast and take on responsibilities that should be just for adults. When I was in the library with her, she kept looking at me as if she wanted me to say something to make everything better.

Adults worry a lot more than they have to about children. I kept thinking I had to make things better for them when they found out about Mum, and that just made things worse for me. I wished they'd just act normal, because when they looked embarrassed I had to say things to make them feel OK, and I didn't always know how to do it. Trying to make things better for Dad was not so bad, but trying to make things better for adults who you don't really know was very annoying, and it made me tired.

After dinner, Dad got up to do his walking. He did walk round the back of the sofa without holding on, but he stumbled and nearly fell. He looked disappointed, but I was very pleased. He was on his feet for twenty minutes, and I wrote it in my notebook. "You're definitely getting better," I told him.

He smiled. "Perhaps not this summer, but next summer, you and I are going away on holiday together. I promise you."

"Where will we go?"

"Where would you like to go?"

I shrugged. "I don't know. We haven't been on holiday for years."

"What about the coast? We could go to Cornwall.

There are beautiful beaches down there and it isn't that far away. You could swim all day long. Would you like that?"

It sounded good to me. "Would you still be in your wheelchair, do you think?"

"I hope not, love. I don't think we could manage if I was." He looked sad and it made me feel sad too.

There were quite a few places we couldn't go even in our own town because of not being able to get the wheelchair inside some buildings. It was mostly the older ones that had big stone steps. We couldn't go to the cinema and we couldn't get inside the café on Merchant Street. That reminded me of the Seepings again. I wondered if Vaquita had a bed in the bathroom or if she had a sleeping bag on the floor.

"What do you think it would be like if you just lived in a bathroom and nowhere else?" I asked Dad.

"I expect you'd be very clean all the time," he said. I could see he was trying not to laugh.

"Our bathroom's too small to have a bed in it, isn't it?"

"Are you getting tired of your own room?"

"No. I was just wondering, that's all. How far away is Cornwall, Dad?"

"About two or three hours from here. We could stay in a hotel close to the sea."

"I wish we could go this year."

"So do I, but I don't see how we can, just the two of us."

He was right. Sometimes when I had to push him in his wheelchair down the street it was almost too hard, and other grown-ups had to help us up kerbs and things.

"Do you think Auntie May would come on holiday with us? Then she could help with the wheelchair."

"Auntie May's back isn't strong. I don't think that would be a good idea. Don't worry; we'll sort something out. Who knows? I might be walking properly by then."

I thought a lot about Vaquita when I was in bed. She didn't really say very much to me. I wanted to find out what she did all day. Maybe she read books or magazines. Maybe there was a TV upstairs. I decided that when I went round to the house again, I'd ask her about the day she left Cotton Street.

I wondered if she was hungry. I didn't see any food in the kitchen at number seven. She didn't look thin or anything. In fact she looked quite round. The swimsuit she was wearing was really old. I'd never heard of someone walking about inside a house in a swimsuit. That was definitely eccentric.

She'd looked as if she needed some fruit. If you're inside all the time and you don't get any sunshine, you

76

can get sick. I tried to remember a history lesson we had about sailors in the olden days and a skin disease they got because they didn't eat fruit. It was called scurvy. We had biscuits and crisps in the cupboard. I decided to take her some, even though she said she liked eating raw things.

I remembered what Mr Lovemore said about telling lies. When he said that hoverflies were pretending to be wasps so that birds wouldn't eat them, and it was one of nature's lies, he was looking straight at me. I didn't know if not telling Dad about Vaquita was a lie or not. Then I thought it probably wasn't, but it still made me feel bad. I think I would've told Mum if she'd been here because Dad said Mum liked Vaquita.

Then I got scared because when Mr Seeping came back, he might find out that I'd seen Vaquita and be angry about it. I didn't know why exactly, except that everything about number seven Cotton Street was a secret. If it wasn't, the front-room curtains wouldn't be closed all day.

Chapter Six

I had a dream about Vaquita. It was a bit complicated because it kept changing all the time. I was walking with her in a field of long grass. It was windy and the grass stems tickled my legs. She was holding my hand, but my hand kept slipping out of hers because it was wet, and sometimes I couldn't keep up with her. First of all she was as big as me, and then she got a lot smaller. She kept saying that we had to run. Then I was carrying her in a plastic bag full of water, and she was very tiny, like a tadpole. But the bag kept trying to slip out of my hands, and I got scared, and so when I saw a puddle in the field, I poured her into it and ran away.

I couldn't really concentrate at school the next day, but my teachers didn't notice. Mr Lovemore wasn't in because his father, who was very old and who'd been ill for a long time, had died.

In English, we had to think about the best holiday

we ever had and then tell everybody. One girl had been to Africa and seen a giraffe crossing the road. The boy next to me had been to the new aquarium on the South coast, and it reminded me of Mr Seeping's fish. I started to think about him again and it made me jumpy. I decided to ask Vaquita not to tell him I'd seen her.

When I had to tell the class about my best holiday, I told them about staying with Auntie May in London when Dad was in hospital. I said we went out every day, and ate in restaurants, and went skating and to the cinema. None of it was true. Auntie May is old, and we didn't go anywhere.

Besides, I didn't want to go out because of Mum just dying. Auntie May gave me some old books to read and some of them smelt and had little yellow spots on the pages. She said she read them when she was my age and that they were true stories. I asked her what a true story was, because I thought all stories were made up. She said a true story was called fact, and a made-up story was called fiction. Auntie May said a made-up story was a bit like telling lies, only the people who read them knew that already and so it didn't matter.

When I got home from school, Mrs Martin was there having a conversation with Dad. They stopped speaking when they saw me, and smiled. Dad said, "We were just talking about you," and then he didn't say anything else.

I went to the kitchen because I knew they were having an adult talk. Mrs Martin had brought us a pot of stew and some jam tarts. I was excited about seeing Vaquita again, but I was slightly scared of everything at number seven now. I ate one of the jam tarts quickly and wondered if I'd be able to make them.

I could hear what Dad and Mrs Martin were saying. Dad said, "He looks white all the time and he can't keep still." I knew he was talking about me. "He says the house is just like ours inside."

"The front garden at number seven used to be lovely before the Seepings moved in," Mrs Martin told him.

"He's only got to go there three more times, then John will be back."

"Danny is a very responsible boy," Mrs Martin said, "compared to some boys."

Dad laughed. "He has to be. But I'm going to make it up to him as soon as I can."

That's when I went back into the sitting room. "I've got to feed the fish now, Dad," I said.

"Shall I come over with you?" Mrs Martin asked.

I went red, but I didn't answer. "Thanks for the stew and the jam tarts."

"Mrs Martin will go with you this time. You can show her the fish," Dad said.

"Are they goldfish?" Mrs Martin asked. "I used to keep those."

I shook my head. "Tropical ones, I expect," I answered. I was feeling annoyed. I didn't think she was interested in the fish at all. I think she just wanted to see what it was like inside number seven. I frowned at Dad.

"Well, shall I just come anyway to check that everything is all right in the house?" she asked.

I wondered if Dad had told her to go with me. "Mr Seeping asked me to make sure the house was all right, as well as feed the fish," I said. "I can do it by myself, thanks," I added.

Mrs Martin shrugged.

"Off you go then. Don't be long," Dad said.

I didn't forget to take some crisps and biscuits. I had them inside my jacket. When I got to number seven, Vaquita was sitting at the top of the stairs looking down at me. She waved and stood up. "When you've fed all those little fishies, come into the kitchen and we can have a talk. I dreamt about you last night."

I was surprised; I didn't know two people could dream about each other at the same time. I nearly told her I'd dreamt about her as well, but I didn't know if

I should because my dream was sad. I didn't think she'd like the idea of being dropped into a puddle in a field.

I found a different favourite fish this time. It was black and white and looked like a triangle, but it took me a long time to decide on it because all of them were special. It was rather like when I go to the sweet shop and look at the different sweets in their jars. People are supposed to know what they want before they go in, otherwise the man in there gets impatient and starts making noises in his throat. But it's too difficult to decide quickly. He's got gummy cola bottles, snowies, mini bears, liquorice comforts, dolly mixture, Haribo yellow bellies, foam teddy bears, sour feet and milk teeth, and that's only the beginning.

I fed the fish and watched them shoot up to the top of the water again, and this time, I put my little finger into the middle tank and some of the fish nibbled me. It made me laugh. Then I remembered that Mr Lovemore told us not to touch or poke things in nature, and I took my finger out again and wiped it on my jumper.

I wondered if Mr Lovemore had ever seen tropical fish – all he seemed to know about was water snails and ponds. Even though the water snails he showed me were handsome like he said, and quite big, they were blackish-brown and a bit dull. I hoped he'd be back at school soon because he was my favourite teacher by far, even if he was eccentric.

Vaquita called me from the kitchen. "Hurry up, Danny Sea-eyes; I've waited all day to talk to you."

When I got to the kitchen, she was sitting on the floor and she looked like she'd just had a bath. The floor was all wet around her. At home, Dad and I didn't have a bath every single day. Dad says it isn't necessary and it's a waste of water. He says people should put their bathwater on their gardens when they've finished with it, especially when there isn't much rain.

I sat down beside her. "I've brought you some crisps and biscuits," I told her.

"Oh, that's kind!" she said, but she didn't take them. "What's your favourite food, Danny?" she asked.

I didn't know the answer. I think that was because I had to cook at home and I didn't always look forward to eating any more. "Mrs Martin's fish pie," I said.

"Isn't that funny? Fish is my favourite food as well."

"Does Mr Seeping like fish pie?" I asked.

"Oh, I don't really know what he likes. He brings me fish though, all kinds of fish."

"I can smell fish now," I said.

"I expect that's because he never opens the windows."

"And never mows the front lawn," I said.

Vaquita looked sad. "There are a lot of things John

doesn't do. It's not his fault. It's because he has to look after me all the time."

"I have to look after my dad all the time too since his accident."

"Matt had an accident?"

"Yes. He's in a wheelchair, but one day he's going to be all right. I'm his carer."

Vaquita moved nearer to me and touched my arm. Her fingers felt very cold. "What about your mum?"

So I told her, and she kept shaking her head and blinking at me. But she didn't get all embarrassed like other grown-ups do. I changed the subject. "Do you watch TV, Vaquita?"

"No, Danny. I don't like the way the pictures move around all the time and won't keep still. It's very annoying."

"Do you read books?"

"What kind of books?"

"Any kind – true stories or made-up stories – fact or fiction."

"I don't have time to read stories, Danny. I'm too busy."

"What do you do all day, Vaquita?"

"I daydream. I think about things. I wait for John to come home."

"Do you see Mr Seeping a lot?"

"I see him every day. What a funny question.

He looks after me."

I wondered if he did look after her properly; her skin looked puffy and blotchy. Then I wondered if I should ask her if she was ill and decided it would be all right. "Do you have some kind of an illness, Vaquita?"

She didn't answer me immediately. Then she said, "I don't think so, Danny," as if she wasn't really sure.

"Then why does Mr Seeping have to look after you?"

She moved away from me a bit. "He likes to because he loves me very much."

"Do you love him too?"

She nodded. "I adore him. I love him so much that when I left Cotton Street to go back to the ocean, I couldn't. I stayed in a little seaside town for a month and sat on the beach every day and thought about him. I was very lonely. Then I came home again, and John made me the fish room. Yet every single day, I think about the real ocean. I wake with the sound of waves in my head and the taste of salt in my mouth. It calls to me all the time, and sometimes I call back. Surely you know that?"

I'm glad she'd told me. "Then you must love the ocean more than anything, Vaquita," I whispered.

"Yes, of course I do," she said. "When were you last there, Danny?"

"When I was little. Dad loves the sea as well. We

85

might go for a holiday in Cornwall next year."

"Do you think your dad would like to go this year?" she asked suddenly.

"I know he would, but we can't. He says another grown-up would have to come with us because of the wheelchair."

"I could go with you," she whispered. "I could help you. I could push the chair. It would be fun."

I didn't know what to say. I had no idea what Dad would think about that. I didn't even know if he really liked Vaquita, he'd never said one way or the other. "I have to go home now. Dad will be worried."

Vaquita stood up slowly. "Will you ask him if we can all go to the ocean together, Danny?"

"Would Mr Seeping come too?" I asked.

She frowned and then shook her head. "Mr Seeping's on holiday right now," she said. "I thought you, me and your dad could go, just to look at the waves for a while, and maybe paddle a bit."

"Would Mr Seeping mind?"

Vaquita sighed. "I don't know."

"Would he be cross if he knew I'd been talking to you when I was supposed to feed the fish and not hang around in here?"

"He might be. He thinks we should keep ourselves to ourselves. He says it's not a good idea to get too involved with other people."

"Then I don't want you to tell him I've seen you, just in case I get into trouble."

By the time I got home, I decided that I really would have to tell Dad about Vaquita. But you couldn't always speak to my dad when you wanted to. You had to wait until he was in a good mood. That was because he got fed up of sitting in his wheelchair. I sat in it once and pretended to be him, but it didn't work. I can't imagine what it must be like not to be able to walk anywhere.

Dad wasn't annoyed with me, but he said I'd been a long time and he was glad I only had to go to number seven twice more. He asked if I'd started writing anything for my project.

"I have to ask Mr Seeping about what it's like living in Cotton Street first, and then write down what he says," I told him.

"He might be lonely," Dad said. "Sometimes lonely people make things up so they don't have to tell you they're lonely."

"No, he isn't lonely, Dad." I shouldn't have said that, it just came out.

Dad looked up at me. "You smell of fish, Danny."

I looked down at my T-shirt. "Number seven is a bit smelly inside," I told him. "Mr Seeping never opens his windows because he's afraid of a burglar getting in and stealing things."

"That'll be why he asked you to make sure the house was all right, then," Dad said. "The Martins have got a key to our house, so when we go away next year, they'll be able to come in and check things for us."

"It's a long time until next year, Dad. Can't we go to the sea this year?"

"Well, I've been talking to the help lady. She said sometimes you can get a volunteer to go on holiday with you."

"What's a volunteer?"

"A kind person who does jobs for other people for nothing."

That's when I could've told Dad about Vaquita, but I didn't know how to begin. I didn't know if I liked Mr Seeping or not. Vaquita's skin wasn't only puffy but it was a bad colour as well, slightly greyish. I kept wondering why he hadn't taken her to a doctor or something. Then I started to feel a bit sorry for him because I thought it would be quite hard to look after her, especially if she was wet all the time.

Dad went around the sofa without touching it once, but he was too tired to do it again. It took him fifteen minutes. I said if he did it once more, he'd have been walking for thirty minutes, the longest time ever, but he shook his head and wouldn't try it. I let him sit down.

"Dad, you know when you don't like someone and

then you change your mind? Does that mean you were wrong in the first place?"

"Who were you thinking of? Not Mrs Martin, I hope. She's been very good to us and you were a bit rude to her earlier."

"It was because I thought she just wanted to see inside number seven. I've heard her say Mr Seeping's strange."

Dad smiled. "I know. You see, the Martins want everybody to be exactly the same as them. At least they think they do. But I reckon if everyone was, it would be boring and they wouldn't really like it at all."

"I wasn't thinking about Mrs Martin anyway. I was thinking about Mr Seeping. You used to like him once."

"So I did, love, so I did," Dad said.

"Anyway, is it all right to change your mind about liking someone?"

"Yes, of course it is."

Chapter Seven

When I got to number seven the next time, I didn't see Vaquita on the top landing. I put my foot on the bottom step and then took it off again. Everything was silent. If Mrs Martin had come with me, I expect she'd have gone straight upstairs. I waited for a while but still didn't hear anything even though I was listening hard. So I called out, "Vaquita! I'm here." There was no answer, so I fed all the fish and sat in the front room pretending I lived at the bottom of the sea. The carpet in there was soft and the colour of sand. I felt miserable and sad, and for a moment, I wished Mrs Martin *had* come with me because she'd know what to do about Vaquita – and I knew something should be done about her.

Then I started wondering if people were still flying kites in the park. The park wasn't all that far away from our house. I decided to ask Dad if I could go and watch them for a while after I'd made our dinner. I'd bought some pizzas with ham and pineapple for a change.

Just as I was about to leave, I heard the strangest sound ever. It wasn't like the first noise I'd heard; it was more like a siren, but gentle. I stared back into the house. The noise stopped for a minute and then started again. I opened the front door and looked out, but it wasn't coming from outside. Something was making a noise inside one of the rooms, but I couldn't tell where it was coming from. It filled the whole house as if the air itself was faintly singing.

Then I heard Vaquita's voice, and my heart jumped. "Danny Sea-eyes, is that you?" she called.

I closed the front door again and looked up at the stairs. "Where are you, Vaquita?"

"In the bathroom," she said. "Come up."

"Am I allowed?" I asked.

"Of course."

My heart was beating very hard. I climbed the staircase slowly. On the upstairs landing, I could see two doors. I knew which one was the bathroom because it was the same as in our house. I knocked on the door and waited.

"Come in, Danny," Vaquita said.

There was a strong fishy smell, and when I opened the door, I knew why. There was a bucket on the floor with some large fish in it. There was an electric heater up on the wall, and it was on, so the room was warm and stuffy.

Vaquita was in the bath, with the water right up to the top. She was lying down, and her chin was resting on the edge of the bath. She still had her old grey swimsuit on. She was smiling at me. "Come in, Danny, and close the door, so the heat doesn't get out."

Everything in number seven was strange, but this was the strangest thing of all. I felt a bit panicky. You don't go into a bathroom when an adult is in there, unless they are your family. Vaquita's arm came out of the bathwater and she spread her fingers out and wriggled them. That was when I wished more than anything my dad could walk. I wished he could run straight into number seven, up the stairs, and get me, because I was frightened.

"I have to go now, Vaquita," I whispered. "I can't stay, Dad's waiting for me."

"Do you really have to? You've only just got here," she said.

I was beginning to feel hot and I couldn't breathe properly. "I didn't really believe you when you said you lived in the bathroom," I told her. "Can I tell you what I honestly think though?"

She blinked at me. "We always used to tell each other honest things," she said.

"Well, it's horrible in this room. The air is all thick and hot, and it smells bad."

"I'm used to it," she said, and she slid down under the water for a minute and then came up again. "You'll find out in time that the world isn't perfect, Danny."

"I already know that!" I said loudly. "I don't need you or anyone else to tell me, Vaquita."

"Sorry," she whispered. "I'd forgotten you've grown up a lot."

She lowered her face for a minute. I could see the top of her head. "Why is your hair so short? It's like boys' hair."

"Short hair is better when you're in the water, and I will be there one day," she said.

"But where do you sleep? I thought you meant you had a bed in here." I stared at the bucket of fish and I had the weirdest idea I'd ever had in my whole life, and it was so peculiar that I felt my face get even hotter. It was only for a second, but I thought Vaquita was not someone you could really call a person.

"Where are all your things, Vaquita – clothes and that?"

"I don't need clothes, Danny."

"You just stay in the bath all the time, don't you?"

"Of course I do, and no one wears clothes in the bath. That would be silly."

"You had clothes once. When you were at the train station, you had a dress on."

"It's true. I did. But I asked John to get rid of all

93

the clothes he'd bought me when I came home again. There's no point in owning things you don't need."

"You said Mr Seeping looked after you, so why do you have to live in the bathroom?"

"It is the best that can be done."

"The other day I thought I quite liked him. Now I'm not sure any more."

"John is a unique man," she said, "and I love him very much."

"I don't think he loves you," I told her.

"Oh, you're wrong there. He loves me more than anything else in the world."

"I don't think my dad would like to think of a person who lived in a bath and had nothing to wear. It would make him quite angry."

"It's not John's fault, Danny."

"Well whose fault is it then? I don't think Mr Seeping looks after you at all."

Vaquita blinked at me again. "It's because I'm a halfling; I belong somewhere else, and he doesn't really know how to look after me properly."

"What did you say?" I crouched down then and looked straight into her eyes.

"I'm half of one thing and half of another thing, Danny Sea-eyes," she whispered. "I thought you knew that already, you certainly *seemed* to know it when you were seven."

"I don't understand you," I said.

"Well, it doesn't matter now. It's your dad I want to talk about. Did you ask him if I can go to the sea with you?" I stared at her. She was like a little child; it was as if she didn't even know how strange she was. "Did you, Danny, did you ask him?"

I shook my head. "Not yet. He doesn't even know you're still in Cotton Street and I don't know how to tell him. He'll be really shocked."

"Are you shocked as well, Danny? Is that why you're looking so angry?"

"I'm angry at Mr Seeping," I told her.

"He's very good to me. Look at the fish he brings me."

"That's what I mean; it's horrible."

"Fish are what I eat."

"Raw?"

She nodded. "Sometimes he has to go for miles to find my favourite ones."

"Nobody eats raw fish."

"Sea people do, and Japanese people do as well, John tells me."

"You're not a sea person, Vaquita, if that's what you're trying to say."

She didn't speak again for a moment, and I stood up to go. "Well, I would be if only I could get to the ocean," she whispered.

"That's stupid. It's not even a good lie," I whispered back. Then I remembered again how she used to tell me stories about sea creatures when I was little, and how real the stories had seemed then. Her fingers were over the side of the bath. I reached out and touched them. "Look, Vaquita, you're just telling me one of your stories, but I'm not small any more and I know the difference between fact and fiction."

I moved away from the edge of the bath. Everything at number seven was too strange. The real reason I was angry and confused though, was that it *had* gone through my mind that I was not looking at a human, but at some kind of other creature. "I'm going to have to tell my dad what you just said, you know," I told her.

"Oh, Danny, please don't be angry with me."

"You're not the only person who wishes they were an animal sometimes, Vaquita. Lots of people do, but they know they're not. I'm going home now. I just want to be somewhere normal," I said.

"Please, Danny, ask your dad to take me to the ocean. I'm ready to go this time," Vaquita whispered as I closed the door and ran down the stairs.

I felt a bit better when I got home, but not much. I wondered about love. I thought that if you loved someone you made sure they were all right. Now, I didn't know any more. Mum and Dad loved each other. Sometimes they used to have rows and things, but not all that

96

much, and anyway they laughed afterwards and hugged, and Dad always kissed the little mole on Mum's cheek.

Dad was in the kitchen in his wheelchair. "I found the pizzas and put them in the oven, but can you get them out again, Danny?"

I was pleased he'd managed it and not waited for me to do it, but I wasn't feeling good. I didn't want to go to the park and see the kites after all. "I'm not hungry. I'm going upstairs."

Dad stared at me and his face fell. "What's wrong?" he whispered. "Something's very wrong, isn't it? I can tell. Come here."

That's when I started to cry and it upset Dad a lot. I hadn't cried in front of him for a long time. "I'm missing Mum," I said. In a way, it was true, but that wasn't why. I just felt confused, and I was angry with Vaquita for telling me a stupid lie and thinking I'd believe her. I tried to remember the word Mr Lovemore had used once when we were talking about snails – gullible; that was it. I wasn't gullible.

"I'm missing Mum too," Dad said. "But I'm getting better every day. Soon we'll be able to go places. Come on, little man. You've got to eat something."

We ate our pizzas at the kitchen table. I kept looking at Dad and wondering if I should say something about Vaquita. But every time I thought I would, I changed my mind. I decided to think about things alone.

"Dad?"

"Yes, Danny?"

"If there was another adult who could go on holiday with us, could we go?"

"Do you know someone who can?"

"I think I do. So can we?"

"Maybe. I'd like that, and I can see you need a holiday. We could go somewhere where there are mountains if you like."

I shook my head. "That's silly. It'd be hard even for an adult to push your wheelchair up a mountain, wouldn't it?"

Dad smiled. "Yes, of course it would be. We could go to the coast then. To the sea, like I said before. Who do you know who could come with us?"

"I'll tell you later, Dad. I've got to think about it first."

Mr Lovemore was back at school the next day, and I was really glad. He had a new yellow jumper on with no holes in it at all. I asked him if I could talk to him at lunchtime in the library, and he said yes. "Sorry about your father dying, Mr Lovemore."

"Thank you, Danny. It was a melancholy business, but he was awfully old, you know."

Community studies was our first lesson. Most people had already started their projects, and some were halfway through. They'd done all kinds of different things to help their neighbours. Some of them had done gardening, others had cleaned people's cars, a couple of the boys had taken their neighbours' dogs for a walk and one girl helped someone mend a shed roof.

I'd fed Mr Seeping's fish and talked to his wife who lived in a bath – his wife who thought she was a sea person. I laughed out loud suddenly, and the class went quiet.

"What's so funny, Danny?" Miss Archer asked.

"Nothing really," I said.

"How are you getting on with your project?"

"It's OK," I answered and looked away.

"What's the job you did?"

"Feeding someone's fish."

"Have you started your written work?"

I shook my head. "I haven't spoken to the man about his life yet."

"You need to get on with it; there are only a couple more weeks, you know. Have you decided on the questions you're going to ask?"

I bit my lip. There was only one question I wanted to ask John Seeping, and that was why his wife thought she belonged in the sea. I nodded my head. "He's a man who likes fish a lot, so I'm going to talk to him about how to keep fish," I murmured.

"That sounds interesting, Danny," Miss Archer said. "What kind of fish are they?"

"Tropical ones," I told her.

"They must be very beautiful. They're not easy to look after. Your neighbour must trust you a lot to let you do it."

I nodded and looked away, and Miss Archer didn't ask me any more questions.

I met Mr Lovemore in the library by the computers. "Could you help me find things out about an animal that lives in the sea, Mr Lovemore?" I asked.

"What animal?"

"I'm not sure. There aren't all that many of them, are there?"

"There are quite a lot, actually. There are sea lions, seals, dolphins, whales, porpoises, walruses, sea otters. Don't you know which one?"

"I've got a feeling I'd know it if I saw it," I told him. "But I don't think it's a whale or a walrus. Maybe a dolphin."

"Is it for schoolwork, or is it something you're interested in yourself?"

"Myself," I said.

"Come on then, let's get started."

We found out all kinds of things about different sea animals and looked at a lot of pictures. We saw wild dolphins, and tame ones as well that play with humans, but they didn't seem to be the right animal. We moved on to porpoises. They don't jump out of the water as much as dolphins do, and some of them are about two and a half metres long. They eat a lot of fish and squid and they can swim fast. Sometimes they get caught in fishing nets and that made me feel sad.

I was feeling like giving up, and then we found one that made me shout out. "This one, Mr Lovemore, this could be it!"

He squeezed my arm. "Shhhh, Danny. We're in the library, remember."

I touched the computer screen with my finger even though you're not allowed to. There were two porpoises in the picture, mostly grey, but with black rings around their eyes and mouths. That's what reminded me of her. You could see sunlight through the water and they were swimming side by side and looking peaceful and happy.

"This porpoise is quite rare," Mr Lovemore said. "There aren't many of them left. Their name means 'little cow' in Spanish. Lovely things, aren't they?"

I stared at the computer screen. "It says their name is vaquita here, doesn't it, Mr Lovemore?" I whispered. I knew it did, but I just wanted him to say so too. The wonderful thing was that they *did* make me think of Mrs Seeping.

Mr Lovemore put his hand on my shoulder. "That's right. Vaquita porpoises. What a life, eh, Danny? Swimming in the sea like that, all happy and free."

I put my head even closer to the computer screen

and read fast under my breath. It said that vaquita porpoises live in shallow murky lagoons in the Gulf of California in Mexico. "Do people capture porpoises sometimes?" I asked. I could feel my chin trembling.

"I'm afraid they do. It's very cruel. They keep them in aquariums and make them do silly tricks. They don't have the space they need to swim about properly. They can't easily be trained; they're not very good at living in tanks, it says."

"How much space do they need, Mr Lovemore?"

"The big wide deep sea," he murmured. "All of it."

I looked down so he couldn't see my face. "It would be impossible to keep one in a bath, then?" I asked.

"Well, these small porpoises would probably just about fit into a bath, but they wouldn't be able to move about and they'd pine for the sea horribly," he said.

"Mr Lovemore?"

"What, Danny?"

"Do you think I'm gullible?"

"Well, it isn't bad to be gullible, Danny, because it means you are able to imagine things, and it'd be terrible to have no imagination, wouldn't it?"

Mrs Brown came over to our computer and frowned at us. "You two, you're talking too loudly; you're disturbing everyone," she whispered.

When we were outside in the corridor again, I looked up at Mr Lovemore and put my hand on his arm because I had to talk to him more and he looked as if he was going to go away. "Yes, but do you?"

"What, Danny?"

"Think I'm gullible?"

He wouldn't answer me properly. "Well, you're a real daydreamer, aren't you?" he said.

"That means I am, doesn't it? I'm just a stupid kid who believes anything."

"I was just the same when I was a boy," Mr Lovemore told me. "I used to play by myself in the forest near our house and invent all kinds of wonderful worlds in my imagination."

"Didn't you have any proper toys to play with?"

"Well, I had some, of course," he said. "But I liked inventing what I needed out of bits of wood and so on. You can change something ordinary into something quite magical just by using your imagination, you know."

"Were your mum and dad very poor?"

"Not at all, Danny. They wanted me to be creative, that's all."

Mr Lovemore went away then, and I stood in the corridor for a while. Everything seemed so strange in my life now. I couldn't work anything out. I just didn't know what to think about Vaquita. For the rest of the day at school, I only pretended to concentrate. I felt numb. I kept looking at the clock and waiting until it was time to go home.

Chapter Eight

Dad and I went to the park on Saturday afternoon. There were a few people with kites there, but the wind was a bit gusty and strong, and they couldn't keep the kites in the air for very long. I sat on one of the benches next to Dad's wheelchair. I had to go back to number seven once more, and this time I *did* want to go. I wanted to look at Vaquita Seeping very carefully. But I couldn't go back there until I'd spoken to Dad about the holiday and what Vaquita had asked.

"Dad, have you ever heard of someone just living in a bath before?" I asked him.

"Don't be silly, Danny, of course not. We had a conversation like this before, didn't we, about bathrooms?"

"No, I'm serious, Dad."

"Are you still thinking about eccentric people?"

"Maybe. But have you ever?"

"No, love, what kind of person would do that?" He

sounded a bit snappy. "Someone who thought they were a fish, maybe? Oh, wait a minute, there was a very famous Frenchman once called Marat who spent a lot of time in his bath and did all his writing there. I expect you'll learn about him when you're older."

I was glad Dad told me that because it made Vaquita seem less weird. "Well, that's all right then," I said under my breath.

Dad patted my knee, and then put his hand on the back of my neck. "Danny, you're so serious these days. Life isn't all that bad. There's going to be a party in Cotton Street tomorrow, it'll be fun."

"Life is bad for some people," I said.

"Maybe it is. But we're all right, aren't we?"

"Dad, you know when you knew Mr and Mrs Seeping before?"

"Yes?"

"Well, what was Mrs Seeping like?"

"Look at that kite, Danny, the red one; it's going to get stuck in that tree."

"What was she like?"

Dad turned to look at me. "How do you mean 'what was she like?'"

"Was she a bit odd?"

"She certainly was."

I wanted to blurt everything out in one go, but I didn't, I was too scared to say it. "Is it possible for a person to be completely mad and yet not really show it?"

"Yes, of course. There were quite a few important people in history who'd fit the bill. King George the Third was one; apparently he gave his pillow a name, and there was a poet called Byron who tried to keep a bear as a pet in his college room. And Marat might not have been completely sane for all we know. But what are you getting at, Danny?"

"I don't think I like Mr Seeping," I answered, to see what he'd say.

"You haven't any good reason not to like him. Well, not at this point in time anyway."

"But you never talk about him properly. Do you actually like him yourself?"

Dad sighed then, and slumped in his wheelchair. "Well, something happened between me and John that I will tell you about one day. I'll tell you when I'm on my feet again, so you're going to have to wait and be patient."

"You don't like him, then."

"I think if Mrs Seeping was still with him, I'd like him a bit more."

I drew in a breath. "Vaquita *is* still with him, Dad. She lives upstairs in the bathroom."

"Good joke, love." Dad laughed loudly and I felt hurt and cross with him.

"OK, then, have it your own way." I looked at the

ground and folded my arms.

Dad touched my shoulder. "Why did you say she's still in the house? What made you think up something like that?"

"Because she is; I've been speaking to her."

Dad touched my arm and when I looked at him, he was smiling at me in a funny way. "I've never seen her on the street. Not once," he said.

"She doesn't go out. But she wants to. She wants to come with us on holiday. She said she could help with things."

Dad's mouth was open and he was silent. Then he said quietly, "I think I'd better come with you to number seven this evening."

Vaquita didn't ask me to bring Dad to the house, and I was worried that if he saw how she was living, he'd get all agitated and then get worse again instead of better. I shook my head. "It wouldn't be a good idea."

"You said she lives in the bathroom. What do you mean, all the time?"

I shrugged. "She lives in the bath, full of water, and only gets out sometimes."

"Holy mackerel," Dad said, and looked down at his hands. "What on earth made you dream up a thing like that? You are a funny boy."

"I didn't dream it up. It's true. She lives in the bath, like Marat."

Dad threw his head back and laughed again, and that annoyed me. "That sounds very strange! I don't suppose you remember her properly from before, though."

"I do remember her properly. She went off to live by the sea and then decided to come home again, and she's been at number seven ever since."

Dad chuckled again. "Is that right?"

"You think I'm making it up," I said.

"So what does she look like, then?"

"Quite small, with grey circles round her eyes." Dad stopped laughing, and I stood up and looked down at him. "I told her I'd let her know if you wanted her to come on holiday. DO YOU?" I shouted at him.

He tried to catch hold of my hands, but I pulled away from him. "Look, how about we go home now, eh? It's a rotten day for kites, and you look tired, Danny."

He wasn't listening to me. "I don't want to go back to Vaquita without an answer. Mr Seeping's coming home tomorrow – if you don't believe me, ask him."

Dad stared at me in a way I'd never seen before. "OK, Danny. Calm down. I'm *not* going to talk to John about Vaquita; it would make him very upset. All I can say is that if Vaquita really *was* still here, I'd be happy for her to come on holiday with us. But she's not."

"She is."

Dad shook his head slowly and looked away from me. "Let's stop this conversation."

"You still don't believe me."

Dad spoke very softly and slowly. "If Vaquita *had* still been in Cotton Street, she'd have been welcome to come on holiday with us."

"Good, then I'm going to tell her she can."

Dad was smiling at me as if the whole thing was a joke. "What are we going to do then, just take her away and not say anything to John, is that the idea?"

He was right, I hadn't thought of that. We had to talk to him first. "Can you ask Mr Seeping if it's OK, Dad?"

"Oh, Danny love, let's not play this game any more."

We didn't talk on the way home. I was angrier with Dad than I'd been for a long time for not believing me. I just wanted life to be simple. I wanted to have Mum again, get up in the morning, go to school, come home, eat dinner. For a while, I hated grown-ups. They didn't tell you things; they expected you to do what they asked, yet they didn't explain anything, and it wasn't fair.

Worse than that, some of them thought you were gullible and told you ridiculous lies. I couldn't wait to get back to number seven. I was going to ask Vaquita some really hard questions, and if she didn't get every single one of them right, I'd know she was just plain batty.

When we got home, Dad put the TV on. He wanted me to sit and watch it with him. I told him I was going upstairs to work on my project, because Miss Archer had said we had to get them finished since school was breaking up for the summer holidays soon. But that's not what I was going to do at all. I waited for a while in my room and thought about Vaquita. Then I went into Mum and Dad's room and closed the door, quietly.

When Mum died, Dad gave away nearly all her clothes and shoes. But there were still a few left. I found her favourite yellow dress in the wardrobe, a red jumper with a zip, and her brown gardening sandals. I put everything into a plastic bag.

I waited until six o'clock and went downstairs. I didn't want Dad to see the plastic bag, so I only opened the sitting-room door a little bit. "I'm going to feed the fish now. I won't be long," I said.

Dad looked as if he wanted to say something important. But he didn't say anything. He just frowned at me.

When I got inside number seven again, I didn't even bother to feed the fish. I went upstairs. I opened the bathroom door without knocking and walked straight in. Vaquita was surprised. I think I frightened

110

her a bit. "Dad says yes," I told her.

She started to grin. I could see her teeth; they were big and square looking. "Oh, Danny, I can't tell you how pleased I am."

"You haven't got any clothes, so I've brought you some of Mum's old things." There was a hook on the back of the bathroom door. I hung the bag up there and turned around to look at her again.

"I'm so excited," Vaquita said. "When are we going?"

"We've got to talk to Mr Seeping first."

Vaquita groaned. "Your dad mustn't say I want to go. Do you understand, Danny? He has to say he *needs* me to go."

I shifted from foot to foot. The air in the bathroom was really stale. "Don't worry, Vaquita. My dad is clever. He'll know what to say. He wanted to come here and speak to you. I said no. Was that right?" I didn't tell her he wouldn't have been able to climb the stairs anyway, and that he didn't believe she was even there; I was trying to make her nervous so I could catch her out with my questions.

Vaquita nodded. "You are so thoughtful, Danny. You are my best friend. I wouldn't really want anyone else to see me in here."

"You don't mind me seeing you though?"

"No, Danny. Not at all."

"Is that because I'm stupid and just believe whatever anyone tells me?"

"No, it's because you're my sea-friend."

"Do you know anything about porpoises?"

She laughed. "What a silly question. Of course I do, I know everything there is to know."

"Really? Did you know that they live right out in the middle of the ocean, they never come near the shore and they only eat seaweed?" Vaquita made a funny blowing sound. I stared at her hard and I had my fingers crossed behind my back. "That's right, isn't it?"

"I don't know who your teacher is, but I think you need to ask for a fresh one, because what you just said is completely wrong."

"And they're not very good at swimming, either," I added loudly. "Did you know that?"

"Come here, Danny Sea-eyes, and I'll tell you something." I knelt on the floor by the bath, even though it was wet. "The place we come from is shallow water and it's a bit muddy. The food we like to eat most is squid because they're easy to catch and very tasty, and how can I not be good at swimming? When we go to the ocean, you'll see that I can, I promise."

I swallowed hard and I could feel my heart beating very fast. "Where exactly is the place you come from?"

"The Gulf of California, by the country of Mexico."

I lowered my head and closed my eyes, and when I opened them again she'd gone right under the water and I couldn't see her properly. I looked at the water for a while and then left the house and put the key back under the stone trout. I stood at the front gate and stared back at number seven. I felt dizzy and strange and I couldn't get my mind working properly. Vaquita knew everything about the little porpoises.

Dad was doing his ankle exercises when I got in. "We are going to talk to Mr Seeping about Vaquita tomorrow, aren't we?" I asked him.

He rubbed his legs and sighed. "Come and sit here, son," he said. "I want to talk to you about Mrs Seeping."

I sat next to him and waited for him to say something else. "You're going to say she can't come, aren't you?"

He shook his head. "Are you missing Mum very badly?"

I nodded. I always missed Mum. That was nothing new; I was used to it. Dad worried about me too much. He must have missed her just as badly. "I thought you wanted to talk about Vaquita," I said.

"Well, I do. Suppose I was to go over to number seven, would I be able to see Vaquita in the same way that you do?"

"You wouldn't be able to get inside the house with the wheelchair. Even if you could, you wouldn't be able to get upstairs."

"Suppose I could walk just like everybody else, and I went into the bathroom at number seven. Would Vaquita really be there?"

"Yes, of course."

Dad stared at me and I stared back at him. "Don't you think John Seeping would be very hurt if we spoke to him about Vaquita when she isn't really in the house at all?"

"I'm not imagining her!" I shouted. "She *is* in the house!"

Dad sighed. "It *is* possible to imagine something so hard that it seems absolutely real," he said.

"You think I'm just a baby, don't you?" I was very angry now.

"I just thought you might be missing Mum so much that you've started to make things up. You know. So you could feel better about everything."

"It's fact, not fiction. She's in number seven Cotton Street right now." Dad frowned at me. I felt like crying. Dad looked as if he wanted to cry too. That's when I decided to tell him everything. I couldn't keep it a secret any more.

"I've worked out that Vaquita thinks she's a porpoise," I whispered.

Dad made a funny noise, like an explosion. "What!" he shouted.

I closed my eyes and put my hands over my ears. "She lives in the bath and eats raw fish."

Dad took hold of my arm. "You're being hysterical, Danny."

"The funny thing is, she really does look like a porpoise if you look at her in a particular way. I went with Mr Lovemore to the library and we did research on porpoises," I said loudly.

I opened my eyes and looked down at the carpet. Then I counted to five in my head and slowly looked up into Dad's face. He was completely white and very stern, and not even his eyes were smiling and his eyes nearly always did smile. He didn't look like my father any more. Then his face creased up, he took me in his arms and pushed my head down onto his chest, and held me for ages without saying anything.

It wasn't until I was lying in bed that I could think properly again, and then suddenly everything was obvious; Mr Seeping himself had told Vaquita all about porpoises, that's why she could answer my questions. There'd been times in my life before when I'd felt disappointed about something, but this time, the feeling of disappointment was so bitter and so strong that it nearly made me cry out. I was disappointed in every single part of my body.

Chapter Nine

Dad was very quiet at breakfast the next morning; he kept looking at me and then looking away again. I couldn't tell what kind of mood he was in. I hadn't slept at all. I'd spent the whole night thinking about Vaquita and what could be wrong with her.

"Look, love," Dad said, "I want to talk to you about yesterday and how bad things got between us. If it would make you feel better, we'll have a bit of a conversation with John today. But if he doesn't mention Vaquita, we won't."

"Fine," I said. "I'm glad. But Vaquita says that we have to tell him you need her to help with the wheelchair, not that she's actually dying to go with us."

Dad made a cross-sounding noise and looked away from me; I could see that he was clenching his jaw. "Let me talk to him first, I need to establish a few things."

"Like whether she's really there or not, I bet,

because you don't believe me."

"Let's not have a quarrel, Danny, please. Just do what I say."

"I'm going to prove she's there. I'm going to find a way of making him say it himself."

By eleven o'clock, there were lots of tables and chairs out in the middle of the road for the party. Mr and Mrs Martin were in charge. There were balloons and ribbons in the trees, and flags going from one lamppost to the other, all the way down the street.

There are hardly any children in our neighbourhood, so most of the people at the party were old. The man who shouts brought his chair out onto the street and watched everything. I don't think Mrs Martin expected him to help. She didn't look at him.

Mrs Malroony was there. She hadn't even got dressed up for the party. She just had on the same old dressing gown that she always wore. She looked very happy. She kept waving at everyone and getting in Mrs Martin's way.

Mr Martin was wearing his black suit, the one he wears to church. But he had a funny hat on as well, it had horns sticking out of it with bells on the end. He looked very silly.

Dad and I were at our front gate. Dad was in his wheelchair and I was sitting on the path next to him.

Cotton Street was blocked off at one end, so cars wouldn't try to drive down. The ice-cream van was allowed to come, though. Dad felt in his pocket for some change. "Want an ice cream, Danny?"

I shook my head. "I didn't really sleep last night. I don't feel well," I told him.

"Nor do I, Danny," he said.

Then Mrs Malroony came to our fence. "Hello my darlings," she said, "have a biscuit." She had lots of biscuits stuffed inside her dressing gown. She felt inside and got some out. They were chocolate and they'd melted.

I looked at Dad and grinned. Somehow, Mrs Malroony seemed normal to me now, compared to Vaquita anyway.

"Thank you, Mrs Malroony," Dad said, "but we've had breakfast. Danny cooked us eggs and bacon."

"Love you," she said. "I'll just leave you some. You can eat them later." She put five biscuits on the pavement in front of our house in a row. Then she shuffled away again.

Me and Dad waited for ages for Mr Seeping to come back. He still hadn't come back by lunchtime. By now, most people in Cotton Street were in fancy dress. One man was dressed like a pirate. He had a real parrot on his shoulder that just stayed there, even though everything was very noisy.

There was another man with a great big nappy on and he did look exactly like a gigantic baby.

Dad nudged me. "What?"

"The man who shouts, look at him," Dad whispered.

He was sitting over the road in his chair in a lady's wedding dress. He had a red wig on that kept slipping when he moved. I stared at him for a long time.

Everybody brought food out and put it on the tables for people to eat. There were all kinds of things: plates of sandwiches, sausage rolls, packets of crisps, chicken drumsticks, meatballs and bowls of salad. Dad told me that Mrs Martin said there'd been a big party in Cotton Street when the war ended, and it was her idea to start them again so people could get to know each other better.

Mr Martin brought out some bottles of lemonade and Coke, and a big stack of plastic cups. Someone had lugged a whole sofa out onto the street for people to sit on if they wanted to. I realized that Cotton Street really was a community. Even if people did gossip sometimes, everybody was laughing and talking to each other now. I wished that Dad and I could feel happy too.

I thought about Vaquita in her bathroom. I felt upset about it. I wondered if she'd looked at the clothes I took her. Then I suddenly felt panicky; I should have asked Dad first, he might feel funny when he saw Vaquita wearing Mum's things. I glanced at him. He was tapping the side of his face and staring down the street.

At about three o'clock, there were some browny-purple clouds in the sky, and everything had gone dark as if it was going to rain hard at any minute. Most of the food had been eaten and there weren't so many people around. The man who shouts helped Mr Martin take down some of the tables, but he did look funny in his wedding dress.

"He was married to someone a long time ago," Dad said. "But she only stayed a couple of months. Perhaps she couldn't stand his shouting. That could be her wedding dress he's wearing."

"Well, it looks like fancy dress anyway," I said. "It looks just as silly as all the others."

"Shhhhh!" Dad said suddenly. "Look!" He pointed down the street and tried to get out of his wheelchair. Mr Seeping was coming. He was walking quite slowly towards us. He stopped to talk to someone for a minute. He ate a couple of the sausage rolls.

Dad gripped onto the fence and got himself out of his wheelchair. He stood up straight and held onto our gate.

My heart started beating.

Dad was staring at Mr Seeping.

I felt the same way I did when I went on a roller-coaster at the fairground once. I was frightened but very excited as well.

I wished I could change everything. I wished Mr Seeping had never asked me to feed his fish. I wished I'd never spoken to Vaquita. I wished I'd never told Dad anything.

Mr Seeping came nearer and nearer. Dad's knuckles had gone white.

"John!" Dad said as he got to our fence.

"Matthew," Mr Seeping said. "I missed the street party. I'd have come home a day sooner if I'd remembered." He put his suitcase down on the ground. I was standing a little bit behind Dad now. "How were the fish?" he asked me.

"Fine, Mr Seeping," I said. I tried to smile at him, but I couldn't.

"I bet you got a big surprise when you first went into the front room, didn't you?"

"Yes, I was amazed," I said. "It's very beautiful in there."

"Good boy," he said. "Thanks for looking after them." He felt in his trouser pocket and brought out some coins. "This is for you."

I shook my head. "I'm not allowed to take any money, because then it wouldn't be doing something for the community," I told him.

"I've never met a boy who didn't need money," he said. "Go on, take it. You don't need to tell your teacher."

"He doesn't want the money, John," Dad said. "He was doing you a favour. Another boy might take it, but not Danny."

Mr Seeping laughed. He took his hat off. It was an old straw one. "Well, I'd never have asked another boy to feed my fish anyway. Danny's the only one I'd trust in my house."

"Was I your first choice?" I asked him.

"I did think of other boys as it happens, but then I knew it had to be you and no one else."

"Oh, why's that, John?" Dad asked. He shifted one of his legs. I thought he was probably getting tired standing up. I moved up to the fence beside him.

Mr Seeping looked away. "Oh, you know what boys are like, can't keep their hands off anything."

"I didn't touch anything," I said.

"I didn't think you would, Danny." He winked at me, and I frowned at him.

Dad straightened his back a bit. "So how was your holiday, John?" he asked.

"It served its purpose," Mr Seeping said. "I went to the new aquarium down on the South coast. I wanted to learn a few things. They have all kinds of marine mammals there. The dolphins were particularly wonderful. They did some fantastic tricks."

"What else was there?" I asked, and I think I already knew.

He smiled at me. "Oh, seals and a big old sea lion."

"And porpoises?"

He nodded. "Yes, they were there too."

"Did they have to do tricks as well, Mr Seeping?" I asked.

"Oh, yes. They jumped straight out of the water and sometimes did back flips."

I waited for a minute for Dad to say something, but he didn't. "Porpoises don't like doing tricks," I said loudly. "They don't like being in tanks. They should be free in the ocean."

Mr Seeping looked at me hard, and then he stared up into the sky and frowned. "Of course they should be," he said quietly. "Of course they should be."

"Do you love porpoises, Mr Seeping?" I asked.

"Doesn't everybody, Danny?"

"Yes, but you love them more than you love people, don't you?"

"Danny, that's enough!" Dad said. "Sorry John, Danny's got himself into a bit of a state."

"No, it isn't enough, Dad. You love porpoises more than you love people, don't you, Mr Seeping?" I asked again.

Mr Seeping went dreamy-looking. "Porpoises are very intelligent, Danny. They're unearthly, graceful –

and forgiving somehow." He looked as if he was going to cry.

"But nobody would keep a porpoise at home, even if they did love them very much," I said. "It would be very cruel, wouldn't it?"

That's when Mr Seeping knew for sure that I'd seen Vaquita. A hoverfly landed on his jacket. He stared down at it and bit his lip. He looked miserable. "I didn't think she'd come downstairs, she said she wouldn't," he whispered. "We talked about it."

"Who?" Dad asked. "Who wouldn't come downstairs?"

"Vaquita, Dad."

Dad shifted his weight onto his left leg. "John?"

"You've got to sit down again, Dad."

"Danny said Vaquita was in the house and I didn't believe him. Are you saying she really is there?"

Mr Seeping ignored Dad. "What did she say to you, Danny?" he asked.

"All kinds of things," I said. I couldn't remember everything we talked about. "She wants to go on holiday with me and Dad."

"My son here claims she lives in the bath, John."

I turned my head quickly and glared at Dad. "I don't *claim* it, I know it!" I said.

"It's true," Mr Seeping whispered. "It's hard to get her out of there."

124

"This is just too fantastic!" Dad said. "I thought looking after me had put Danny under so much pressure that he was beginning to make up absurd stories. Why are you making her live like that, John?"

"I'm not making her. I can scarcely get her to come out of the bathroom. I made the fish room for her to encourage her to come downstairs more. You can even smell the sea there and hear waves, can't you, Danny?"

I nodded. "It's like being under the ocean," I said.

"And you can hear seagulls too, can't you?" Mr Seeping started to cry. I hadn't seen another grown-up except Dad crying before, and it shocked me a lot. Dad sat back down in his wheelchair suddenly. I moved behind him and held onto the handles.

"Well," Dad said, "we've got to do something about this situation, John. Poor Vaquita, how long has she been like this? You should get some help."

Mrs Malroony's biscuits were still lying on the pavement and most people had gone back into their houses. It was beginning to rain, but each raindrop was so tiny that it was a bit like mist.

Mr Seeping looked down Cotton Street towards his house. "There's only one thing that can make it right," he whispered, "and neither of us can bear the idea."

"Get a doctor to see her," Dad said.

"Can we take Mrs Seeping on holiday with us?" I asked quickly.

Mr Seeping shook his head. "She wouldn't agree to go, Danny."

Dad and I looked at each other, and Dad said, "Apparently Vaquita does want to come, John. We're planning a trip to the seaside."

"She said she'd come just to help me with Dad," I added, "since I can't do it alone."

Mr Seeping looked like he didn't know what to do. He kept blinking back his tears. I felt like crying too, but I didn't. I'd been frightened about us meeting him at first, but I wasn't any more.

"Why don't you come with us, John?" Dad asked. "We could start playing chess again, put things right between us. It's about time."

"That's a very generous and extraordinary offer," Mr Seeping said. He glanced at me quickly. "Given what happened. I won't come though."

"But can Mrs Seeping come?" I asked. "Please let her. We really do need help with the wheelchair," I told him.

"Are you prepared to take my wife to the coast, Matthew?"

"Yes, we'll take her. I'll try and talk to her, maybe it'll help."

"And I'll go swimming with her," I said.

I'd never seen anyone look as sad as Mr Seeping did at that moment. He stared at my face for a long time before he said anything else. Then all of a sudden, he smiled. "Take her then. She'll come back. I'm sure she will," he said, and picking up his bag, he walked away from us very slowly towards number seven Cotton Street.

Chapter Ten

The next day Dad kept saying, "Poor John, if only I'd known sooner. I could have helped him."

"Poor Vaquita as well," I said in the end.

"We're going to have to be very gentle with her."

"Do you think she's even battier than Mrs Malroony?"

Dad laughed, but he didn't sound happy. "I don't know, Danny. Life is strange, isn't it? Let's just see what happens."

"Why did Mr Seeping think she wouldn't come downstairs and find me?"

Dad thought for a minute. "Maybe he really did want her to find you. In his heart."

"Like an on-purpose accident, you mean?"

Dad nodded. "I think so. He can't go on living like that any more."

I felt better than I'd done for ages. Dad was looking

at holiday magazines to try to find the best place for us with the wheelchair. I had one more week at school before the holidays. We had to hand our community studies project in. I hadn't written anything and I didn't know what to do. That was the only thing that was worrying me now.

Dad said I'd still have time to do it.

"I don't want it to be Mr Seeping, though," I said. "I'm scared he'll change his mind about Vaquita if I ask him questions about his life in Cotton Street."

Dad nodded. "I think you're right there. Imagine what it must be like for him living with Vaquita."

"What's a halfling, Dad?"

Dad shrugged. "So who are you going to choose for your project?"

"I might still have time to interview Mrs Martin," I said, "but I haven't done a job for her, and I don't know what to ask her about."

"Ask her how Cotton Street has changed. Get her to tell you what it used to be like in the old days," Dad said.

"Yes, but I haven't done any jobs for her."

"Well go and ask her for a job. Go on. Do it now."

So I went over to the Martins' house and Mrs Martin said I could help her in the garden. Her garden was very small, like ours. We did weeding and watering.

"What was Cotton Street like in the olden days, Mrs

Martin?" I asked her. She laughed a bit. She was quite old, so I asked if she'd forgotten.

"Oh no, I haven't forgotten. You don't forget things like that."

She said that people in Cotton Street always kept their front doors open in the summer. "But that's silly, Mrs Martin. Anybody could just walk in and steal everything."

She smiled. "No. In those days, everybody knew each other and everybody helped each other in Cotton Street. We had a big street party just after the war. Do you know about the Second World War, Danny?"

"Only a little bit," I said. "Lots of places got bombed, didn't they?"

"That's right. A few houses on Cotton Street did as well." She sighed. "If you didn't leave your front door open in those days, people thought you were trying to hide something."

"But that means you *had* to do it even if you didn't want to," I said.

"Maybe. But we wanted to do it to show we trusted people. There are often two sides to something. Something can be good and bad all at the same time."

"Did people leave their curtains open, as well, in the war?" I was thinking about number seven and how Mr Seeping never opened his curtains.

"Goodness me, no! You see because of the war,

130

we had to keep everything very dark at night, so the enemy aeroplanes couldn't work out where Cotton Street was and bomb us. If there was even a tiny bit of light showing we could get into trouble."

"Wow."

"One of Mr Martin's jobs was to go down Cotton Street after dark and make sure no light was showing through people's curtains."

"What did he do if there was?"

"He used to knock on their doors very loudly, and then tell them off. People had to be a real community then, you see."

"Who lived at number seven, Mrs Martin?"

"Mr Seeping's house? I think it was a family, but the children were sent away to the countryside to keep them safe. The front garden always looked nice. There used to be flowers and butterflies everywhere."

"It doesn't look very good any more," I said.

"No, it doesn't. Mr Seeping is a bit odd, if you ask me. But I do feel sorry for him being alone like that."

"Our garden is quite nice. But we don't get many butterflies, only white ones," I said.

Mrs Martin sighed. "That's something that's changed in Cotton Street. All the butterflies have gone."

"Mr Lovemore at school says that lots of insects are dying out now because we don't take care of them.

He said that some moths look just the same as the trees they live on, and other insects, hoverflies for instance, pretend to be poisonous so that birds don't eat them. Do you think some people could be like that, Mrs Martin?"

"Pretending to be what they're not, do you mean?" She laughed. "Well, all kinds of people might try to pretend to be something they're not, but they don't fool us, do they?"

"No, Mrs Martin, they don't fool us one bit. We aren't that gullible."

She told me lots of things about what Cotton Street used to be like and later I wrote down what I could remember. She said something could be good and bad at the same time. I never knew that before, and when I thought about Mr Seeping, I thought it was good that he loved Vaquita so much, but there was also something bad about it.

At school, Miss Archer said everybody had done very good projects. She said she was proud of us. But after the lesson, she made me wait behind.

"Danny."

"Yes, Miss Archer?"

"About your project. You had some good ideas in it. What you wrote was very interesting. But it looked terrible – your handwriting was sloppy, there were smudges on the paper. You weren't at all careful about it, were you?"

"No, Miss Archer."

"I gave you a good mark, because I know that things are tough at home."

"Yes, Miss Archer."

"How is everything these days? How's your dad doing?"

"OK, Miss Archer."

"You look as if you have the weight of the world on your shoulders, young man. Are you going on holiday when we break up?"

"Yes, Dad and I are going to stay in Treganeth. That's in Cornwall." I nearly said something about Vaquita, but I decided not to.

"Well, have a good time, won't you? Forget about everything for a while."

"Yes, Miss Archer."

Then school was finished for the summer. I woke up really early on the morning of our holiday because I had to make sure the house was clean enough for Dad. I hoovered the stairs and the sitting room. Dad wanted me to clean the top of the stove. I didn't want to do it, but I didn't complain; I just did it.

I made us some breakfast and packed Dad's bag and my backpack. We were going to go to a hotel called the New Regina, by coach, and Dad said we should take something to eat because it would be a long journey. I made some cheese and tomato sandwiches for Dad and me and tuna-fish sandwiches for Vaquita, because that's what I thought she'd probably like.

Dad had a long talk with me that morning. I didn't contradict him about anything, and for the hundredth time since the street party, he apologized for having doubted me about Vaquita.

"When we get to the hotel, Danny, I'm going to have to spend some time talking to her, and it'll be a bit boring for you. She's got herself into a bit of a mess, and I'm going to try and help her work out what to do."

"Yes, Dad."

"When she's away from Cotton Street, she might see that she does have choices in life and that she doesn't have to live in a bath all the time."

"As if she was a porpoise."

"Has she actually said that to you?"

"Not in words, but she knows everything there is to know about a particular kind of porpoise."

Dad pulled me close to him. "Well, anyway, as long as you have fun, that's all that really matters, love."

At eleven o'clock, I wheeled Dad down to the Seepings' house, and as we got to the gate, we saw Vaquita. She was standing outside the front door dressed in Mum's clothes. My heart started beating again. I'd forgotten about them.

We didn't go through the gate. I waved at Vaquita and she waved back. Mum's yellow dress was far too long for her.

I waited for Dad to say something, but he didn't. He waved at Vaquita. "It really is her," he said. "I can hardly believe my eyes."

Vaquita picked up her little suitcase and started to walk down the garden path towards us. That's when Mr Seeping opened the front door. He looked awful. I could see he was shaking even from where we were standing. Vaquita put the suitcase down and walked back to him. Dad and I watched.

Mr Seeping put his arms around her and hugged her. They stood like that for a long time. He kept putting his head down into her neck and rocking her from side to side. Then he dropped his arms suddenly and stepped back.

I could see Vaquita shaking her head. She was wearing Mr Seeping's straw hat.

"I wish she'd hurry up, Dad," I said.

"Let them say goodbye, Danny. Sometimes good-bye can take a very long time."

Then Mr Seeping turned round and walked back inside. He shut the door and Vaquita stood looking at the house for a while. I didn't know if I should call her or not. Dad said to wait.

In the end, she picked up her suitcase and turned

round very slowly and started walking towards us. I realized I was holding my breath.

"What on earth!" Dad said. "Look what she's wearing. A dress just like Mum's."

I had to tell him. If I hadn't it would've spoilt things. "I gave it to her, Dad. She didn't have any clothes, just a horrible grey swimsuit."

Dad made a funny noise. By then Vaquita was right in front of us. She kept squinting and blinking. She was smiling too, but there were tears on her cheeks.

"Good to see you again, Matt. It's been a long time," she said. She looked at me and smiled. "My most best friend ever," she whispered. "Danny Sea-eyes Broadaxe."

"You look great, Vaquita," I said, even though she looked awful.

"Let's go before I decide not to," she said. She turned round once again and looked at the house. I thought she might suddenly change her mind, so I opened the gate quickly and took her hand. I was shocked; her fingers felt as cold as ice.

We began to walk to the coach station. Dad said we should take the shortcut so it wouldn't take as long. But I think it was really so that no one saw us. He didn't want to go all the way up Cotton Street again so that everyone could look out of their windows and watch us.

I suppose we did look funny. Dad was holding Vaquita's suitcase and his bag on his lap. I was wearing my backpack and pushing Dad, and Vaquita was walking beside me. She seemed to roll from side to side. She kept looking round at everything. She moved very slowly.

"What time is our coach, Dad?" I asked.

"Don't worry, Danny. It isn't until twelve. We have plenty of time."

I was relieved.

Vaquita kept saying, "My goodness, look at that!" She said it about almost anything. She said it about lampposts, trees, people's houses, everything.

"It's been a while since you were outside, Vaquita," Dad said. "It must be like seeing things for the first time." He spoke in a whisper and he sounded very gentle.

"Oh, Matt, it is. That's the trouble when you have so much housework to do. You just don't go out."

I turned my head to look at her. Vaquita didn't do housework. I wondered if she was going to tell lies all the time we were on holiday.

"Danny complains about how much work he has to do in the house as well."

I felt cross for a minute. "No, I don't Dad. That's not fair," I said. "Well, only sometimes."

* * *

137

The driver helped Dad onto the coach and I tried to fold up the wheelchair. I'd done it once or twice before, but it was difficult. Vaquita tried to help, but she wasn't any good at it either. The driver worked out how to do it, and he put it in the space for luggage that's in the side of the coach.

Vaquita was nervous, she kept laughing all the time at nothing. She didn't want to sit down. I was embarrassed. She was just like a kid. Dad told us to sit behind him and to be quiet for a while. He looked tired, but I think he was pleased to be going on holiday. Then he fell asleep.

It took ages and ages to get to Cornwall. Vaquita slept for a while and when she woke up again she made a funny puffing noise. She turned her head to look at me and I thought she seemed a bit scared. Then she smiled. "Do you remember me telling you that I had a dream about you, Danny?" she asked.

"Yes, I do."

"I dreamt that we went swimming," she said.

"Oh! Did you bring your swimsuit, Vaquita?" I asked.

"Of course. It's in my suitcase. I dreamt that we swam through beautiful green waves. We swam on and on and on; we swam for miles. The water was cold for a long time. Then it got warmer, and shallower." She smiled at me. "Until finally we were in delicious thick water."

"Thick water?"

"Yes, Danny, where the water is full of life and mud and warmth."

"I had a dream about you as well," I said. "Everything in my dream was green too, because we were in a field. My dream wasn't as nice as yours." I didn't want to tell her about the puddle.

She blinked at me. "Then in my dream the water was very shallow, and we ate so many fish and squids that we felt as if we were bursting. After that, we both went to sleep."

"Did we have a barbecue?" I asked her.

She shook her head. "Oh no, Danny. We were just catching the fish and eating them straight off."

I pulled a face. "I wouldn't like to eat them raw," I said.

Dad woke up then. "Japanese people eat fish raw," he said.

"Told you," Vaquita whispered. She giggled.

"Can we have fish and chips for dinner tonight, Dad?"

"Of course we can, Danny. If you're hungry now, eat the sandwiches you made."

We got to Treganeth at three o'clock and when the driver had helped Dad get into his wheelchair again, we looked around. The streets were narrow and they all led down to the sea. There were shops that sold buckets and spades and sunglasses. There were other shops that sold postcards and model sailing ships, and there were tons of cafés and restaurants. Some of the buildings looked ancient and they had crooked roofs and tiny windows and great big chimney pots.

From where we were standing, you could see the sea. It looked blue and grey at the same time. You could smell it as well. Vaquita kept standing on one foot and then the other, and saying, "Look at the water, Danny, look at it."

Dad stared at her with his head on one side. He was grinning. So was I.

Chapter Eleven

The New Regina Hotel was right on the seafront. It was easy to get Dad inside because there weren't any steps and the doors were glass and slid open when you got to them. We went to the man behind the desk. I pushed Dad and Vaquita followed us. The man didn't say anything, he kept glancing at Vaquita and then at my dad all the time. He looked at me as well and frowned.

Dad said, "Broadaxe, two rooms."

Vaquita took Mr Seeping's straw hat off and the man stared at her. He probably thought her hair was horrible.

"We booked rooms here," I said.

I could see that the man didn't know who to talk to. Then he looked down at Dad again and shouted, "Mr Broadaxe, two rooms, one with a bathroom?"

"Why is he shouting?" Vaquita asked. "We're not late, are we?"

Dad laughed. "He thinks I'm deaf," he whispered. "There are still a few people who shout at anyone in a wheelchair."

"Very rude," Vaquita whispered back. She went right up close to the man and leant over his desk. "Do the rooms have a view of the sea?" she shouted loudly, right into his face.

Dad and I grinned. I loved Vaquita for doing that.

When I'd unpacked Dad's stuff and my stuff, I went to Vaquita's room. "Dad said we should have some tea before we do anything else," I told her. "He's downstairs waiting for us."

She was running a bath and the water was quite near the top. "Oh, do we have to, Danny?"

"I think Dad's tired and hungry," I said. "It wasn't comfortable for him on the coach."

"You go down. I just need to lie in the water for a bit."

"Please come, Vaquita. Dad would really like it if you did," I told her. "It would be rude not to."

We found Dad in the dining room at a table by the window. There was nobody else in there. The sea wasn't far away from the hotel, and the waves looked quite big. I noticed there were a few very black clouds on the horizon, and I hoped that didn't mean it was going to rain. Vaquita kept standing up and then sitting down again. She wouldn't have any tea or cake. Then she started wandering around the room and touching the walls. It was quite dark in the dining room and there was a big chandelier hanging from the ceiling.

"She's just a bit excited, Danny. She'll calm down in a while," Dad whispered. "I'm not sure how to start talking to her though."

"Ask her what a halfling is."

Dad turned his head to look at her again. She was running her fingers down the windowpane and she looked very restless. "I feel terribly sorry for her. She's got a jumper on under that dress, hasn't she?"

I nodded. "It's Mum's red one with a zip," I told him. "You're not angry that I gave her Mum's clothes, are you, Dad?"

"When I saw her coming out of number seven in your mother's dress, I did feel shocked. But it doesn't really look anything like it did on your lovely mum."

I felt tears come into my eyes, and Dad noticed. He squeezed my hand and smiled. "I'm tired now," he said. "Why don't you go for a walk with Vaquita while I take a nap?"

Vaquita and I both wanted to go to the beach and look at the waves, so that's what we did. It was about six o'clock in the evening. Nobody was on the beach then. The clouds were bigger and they looked very heavy and dark grey. When we reached the sand, Vaquita took

Mum's sandals off and ran towards the water.

"Wait for me," I called. I picked up the sandals and followed. I was cross with her.

"Look, Danny," she said, "it goes on for ever. Let's go in now. This is just like the dream I had."

"We can't, Vaquita. Dad said we could swim tomorrow."

She made a funny puffing noise and frowned at me. Then she looked back at the hotel. "Matt *was* very kind to bring me here," she said. "I suppose it would be rude to leave right away."

"I thought you said you wanted to come to help me with Dad," I said. "You haven't really helped at all."

"Sorry, Danny. You're right. I've only been thinking about myself."

Then she sat down on the wet sand at the edge of the waves and Mum's dress got soaked. The sea water ran all over her legs. I was worried. I thought we should go back to the hotel and make sure Dad was OK.

"Do you like my dad, Vaquita?" I asked her.

"Why do you ask?"

"Because he wants to help you. He thinks you're confused about things."

She looked up at me. I was standing behind her a bit, so my trainers didn't get wet when the waves came in. "Your dad's a nice man. I do like him, and I'm sorry for him because of his legs and because of your mum."

144

"Do you remember my mum, Vaquita?"

"A little bit. She had green eyes like yours, all sparkly and happy, and a little black thing on her left cheek."

I put my hand to my own left cheek. "Trouble is, I keep forgetting things about her," I said, "and it makes me feel bad and guilty."

"None of us wants to let go of the ones we love, Danny."

"I didn't *let* go of her, that's the whole trouble; she was taken away from me. I've told you that already. A man crashed into Dad's car, his legs got crushed and she died."

"What happened to the one who did it?" Vaquita asked me gently.

"I don't know. Dad says it's best not to keep on thinking about it. He says he's sure he feels terrible because of it."

A wave came in that was bigger than the other ones; I moved away. But Vaquita lay back on the sand so that the water went right over her body. She was completely wet. She had her eyes closed. Now we had to go back to the hotel with her dripping on the big red carpet, and the man behind the desk would see us. We might even get chucked out. "We have to go back now," I said. "Dad will be worried, and I think it's going to rain."

I was surprised when she stood up. I had expected her to say no. "All right then, we'll wait for tomorrow. Everything will happen tomorrow."

"And will you answer my dad properly if he asks you things – and not mind about it?"

"I will, Danny. I promise."

We did have fish and chips for dinner that night, but Dad and Vaquita hardly ate anything. I could tell Dad was about to have a serious talk with her, so I didn't speak.

"Are you glad you came, Vaquita?" he asked.

"I am so grateful to you both," she answered. "To Danny Sea-eyes for always understanding me, and to you, Matt, for bringing me here. Although this isn't a beach I've ever swum to before."

"Swum to?" Dad repeated. "Swum from, you mean."

"No. Swum to. I don't remember ever swimming to this place from anywhere."

Dad chuckled, and Vaquita beamed back at him, showing her big square teeth. "What is a halfling exactly?" he asked her in a very gentle voice. I thought he'd forgotten about that.

"It's someone who is half one thing and half an-other."

"Is that right?" Dad asked, and Vaquita couldn't see

that he was humouring her. "And does that mean the person is not one thing, nor the other?"

"No, the person is both. BOTH. And it's not funny, Matt, it's tragic." Vaquita looked away from us.

"I apologize, Vaquita," Dad said, looking serious again. "It's just that we're worried about you. Normal people don't live in baths. Have you thought about what it does to John?"

"I think about it every day," she whispered.

"Would you be prepared to see a doctor when we get home, if not for your sake, for John's?"

Vaquita stared down at her plate, and then straight at me. There were quite a few people in the dining room now, and Dad kept looking round to make sure they weren't listening to the conversation. The whole sky had turned dark by then and the first flash of lightning came and lit up Vaquita's face for a second. She looked wild and strange.

I was bursting to say something to her even though I was supposed to keep out of things. "What exactly is it you think you are, Vaquita?" I asked her.

She got to her feet suddenly and stared at us both. Her eyes filled with tears and they ran down her cheeks very fast. "John knows what I am. He's always known."

"Sit down, Vaquita," Dad whispered, "people are looking." She sat down slowly and wiped her face on her serviette. "I don't know how you two got your-selves into such a strange situation, but you could live a normal life again if you wanted to."

"Could I?" Vaquita asked.

"Of course you could. It's up to you. You just have to make the decision to change things."

"Shush, Dad," I whispered, "you're shouting." There was a tableful of people at the other end of the dinning room who kept looking at us.

"If John's a kind man, I can't think he wants you to go on living like this either," Dad said.

Vaquita stared out at the black clouds. "John didn't say I had to *promise* to come back. We had a long talk before I left," she murmured.

"Maybe you and Mr Seeping could move down here, then you could swim in the sea whenever you wanted, because that's what you really like most, isn't it?" I asked.

"Of course it is, Danny. I pine for the ocean terribly."

I remembered what Mr Lovemore had said in the library. "You'd have the whole wide deep sea," I whis-pered. "All of it."

Vaquita started to smile. "A long swim is what I need, and I'll be as good as new."

Dad looked pleased. "Good," he said, "and that's what you will have tomorrow."

* * *

148

I was glad when we all went upstairs to bed. I was tired. But I couldn't sleep because Dad was snoring and my blankets were itchy and too tight. I felt sorry for Vaquita because I thought it was all right to invent imaginary worlds when you were just a child, but not when you were supposed to be a grown-up like she was.

Just then, I heard a lovely sound that was soft and sharp at the same time, like half wailing and half singing. I couldn't tell where it was coming from. I got out of bed and went to the window. There were a few cars in the street and a couple of people. The waves were huge and the darkness made them look black. I could see their white edges as they hit the beach. A moment later I realized it was Vaquita making the sound.

I was shaking as I walked into her room. It was dark in there, but there was a light on in the bathroom. "Vaquita!" I said, trying to keep my voice low.

The sound stopped immediately. "In here, Danny," she said.

She was lying in the bath with only her head above the water. The floor was soaking wet. "Stop making that noise," I said. "You'll wake everybody up, and then we might get chucked out."

"I was singing a song of joy and lament, Danny," she said. "Because I am happy and sad at the same time."

149

"Well be happy and sad in the morning. I don't want Dad waking up, otherwise he'll be irritated tomorrow."

I didn't wait for an answer. I closed the door and went back to our room.

In the morning, Dad was cheerful and Vaquita was very quiet. She kept looking through the window towards the sea. We had kippers for breakfast and she ate hers fast. This time she had Mum's jumper on top of the yellow dress and she looked a lot better that way. I noticed the strap of her grey swimsuit under the dress. I had my trunks on under my trousers, too. I smiled at her. I could tell she was bursting to get down to the sea again, and so was I.

There were only a few people on the beach when we got there because it was still early. Vaquita and I had to push Dad over the sand together. It was really hard because the sand was so dry. We parked him quite high up on the beach, away from the water.

Dad had brought a newspaper with him. "Go on then," he said to us both, "swim to your hearts' content. I'm going to read. Danny, don't go in further than your chest, OK?"

"OK," I said.

"No, come here." Dad took hold of my arms and looked hard into my face. "I said don't go in further than your chest, and I really mean it."

"I heard you, Dad. Don't worry."

Vaquita stood beside me and took my hand. "Trust me, Matt," she said in a very soft voice. "I'll look after Danny Sea-eyes."

Dad gazed at her. "I wish I could go in with you." Then he laughed. "Well, I wish I could *walk* first, of course."

Vaquita bent down and kissed Dad on the cheek, and he looked really surprised, but pleased. He raised his fingers to the place she'd kissed him and smiled.

We left Dad to read and walked together down to the sea. The water looked beautiful. It was sometimes green and sometimes grey with bits of blue in it. It wasn't exactly hot that day. There was a cool wind and some fast-moving clouds, and the waves were as high as they'd been the day before.

"Let's not waste any time, Danny," Vaquita said.

We took our clothes off and dropped them on the sand. I looked round to see if Dad was OK. He was reading his newspaper, and by the time I turned back to say something to Vaquita, she wasn't there any more. She was running into the water, fast.

"Wait for me!" I called out, but she didn't hear me, so I went straight in after her. But by the time the water was up to my waist, I saw her dive under a big wave.

I swam a bit more, but the waves were strong. I kept stopping and trying to stand up, but I got knocked about a lot. When the water was up to my chest, I looked around.

Suddenly Vaquita came up next to me, almost out of nowhere. "Come under with me, Danny. It's so beautiful and still below."

Before I could decide, she grabbed one of my hands and took me under the water with her. I only just had time to take a big breath. The salt water went straight up my nose. Vaquita was right though; it was peaceful under the water. The bottom was sandy and the sunlight was making patterns on it. There wasn't any seaweed or rocks.

She still had me by the hand, so I let her take me with her. It was very dreamy down there. When my lungs began to hurt, I pulled my hand out of hers and got my head back out of the water. I looked over to where Dad was sitting.

Vaquita came up quickly beside me. "Don't worry about your dad," she said.

"I'm just making sure he's all right," I told her. "I have to."

"You can't forget about him for one minute, can you?" We were face to face, treading water. "Soon you'll be able to," she told me. "Come back under for a while."

So, we went under again. This time she rolled over and over with her arms close to her body. I tried to do the same thing, but I couldn't. Even under the water, I could see that she was smiling. She came towards me swiftly, and suddenly I was holding onto her shoulders and we were moving so fast through the water that I couldn't believe it. She could swim all right!

I held onto her and kept my body close to hers. Then I realized she'd changed direction; we were moving towards the deep water. I kicked her with my heel. That made her go up to the surface again. I was clinging to her and coughing hard. We were a long way from the shore and I was beginning to get scared. I could only just see Dad.

"I'm not supposed to be out here," I said. "Take me back."

Vaquita started to swim back slowly beneath the water, close to the surface. I held onto her very tightly. I had my head out of the waves and I could breathe again. She never came up for breath once. For a long time it was as if there was only Vaquita and me in the whole world.

Chapter Twelve

When we got close to the beach again, I let go of her neck. I could feel my heart beating.

"Didn't you like it, Danny?" she asked.

"I loved it, but I'm not allowed to go into deep water," I told her, "you know that." My voice sounded scratchy. I could see Dad properly again now and I felt better.

Vaquita stretched her neck up and looked towards him. "Your dad loves you very much, doesn't he?" she asked.

"Yes. I love Dad very much too."

"Are you going to live with him for ever?"

I coughed and it hurt my throat. "No, not my whole life, obviously."

She rolled over and then back again. "Same for me," she said. "I can't live with John all my life either, as much as I would like to. Talking to your dad last night made me realize that it isn't John who has to decide, but me."

I didn't know what she meant, but when I first saw her in the bathroom at number seven, she looked tired and sad. She wasn't like that any more. She glistened all over. She seemed very strong. The sun went behind a cloud and it made her look grey. She flipped over again and moved quickly beneath a wave. I waited to see her come up, but she didn't. Then I saw her head just poking out of the water a long way off. I waved at her, and the next thing I knew she was beside me again.

She blew some bubbles in the water. "I know somewhere warmer than this. A place full of fish," she said. "Would you like to go there?"

"Like in your dream, you mean?" I asked her.

"Just like that. Come with me, Danny Sea-eyes, and I'll show it to you."

She moved further out so the waves didn't crash on her all the time. When we were in our room the night before, Dad had told me he didn't think she'd want to swim for long. "She doesn't look well, and there might be underwater currents, so keep your eye on her," he said.

I swam to her and she took hold of my hands and started to pull me along. She held me gently, and my legs floated out behind me. "I think you're ready now," she said after a while.

"For what?"

"We're going to Mexico."

"Oh, *are* we?" I said. We grinned at each other. "I love playing with you; I wish we could do it all the time."

She kissed me once on the cheek and then said, "Put your arms around my neck, take a very deep breath and hold on tight."

I did as she asked and we went under together, and within a couple of seconds, I knew two things; we were moving into deep water again at a terrible speed and she was no longer a human being. Her body had become rounded. Her cool skin against my face and arms was rubbery and smooth.

Vaquita Seeping *was* a porpoise. I could feel the power of her body beneath my fingers and I started to tingle all over with excitement. We were further down now where the water was colder and darker, and she wasn't moving as fast. A long piece of brown seaweed wrapped itself around my arm, but I had to leave it there because I was afraid to let go of her even with one hand. I saw a cloud of silver fish swimming to-gether close by. I sensed that Vaquita had seen them too, although she didn't try to get them. It was as if she knew exactly where she was heading for and noth-ing was going to put her off. It was only then that I realized we were not playing at all, but travelling, and

I began to feel frightened – so frightened that I wanted to open my mouth and cry out, but I couldn't. My ears were hurting badly and there was an ache in my chest. I hit her with the side of my foot, but she didn't seem to notice.

I was terrified of letting go of her, and even more frightened of not letting go of her. Yet in the end I had no choice; I had to be free because my lungs felt as if they were on fire. I felt myself drifting upwards to the surface and I kicked hard to speed myself up. I could see shimmering light high above me, but it was so far away I knew I wouldn't get there before my lungs burst.

I thought about Dad. I thought about him harder than I ever had before. Mum was there too, and I remembered things I'd forgotten long ago. I remembered the day she showed me a tiny wren in a hedge, and told me to be very still in case we frightened it away. I remembered the feeling of her hand on my back as she crouched beside me, and how warm the air was. The light at the top of the water was no closer, and that's when I knew what loneliness was really like. Then suddenly Vaquita was with me. She pushed me fast through the water with her big blunt head and nudged me into the shallows where I could feel the bottom with my feet, and my face was finally in the air again.

The first thing I saw when I stopped gasping for breath was my dad. He was standing up beside his wheelchair. Then he was walking and sometimes trying to run. He looked stiff and funny, but he was coming towards us. His face looked pale and wild. He fell over once in the sand and got up again. He was waving his arms about. I could see his mouth moving, but I couldn't hear what he was saying.

I made my way through the waves to the beach as fast as I could. Sea water was coming out of my nose and my lungs were still hurting. My legs felt like jelly as I got out of the water.

When Dad reached me, he sat down heavily in the wet sand, and then stood up and put his arms around me. I was shivering. He tried to dry my hair on his T-shirt. "Danny, Danny, Danny!" he murmured.

"I'm all right, Dad."

"Where's Vaquita?" He moved away from me and stared at the ocean, shading his eyes from the sun. I wanted to tell him, but I couldn't find the words. "Did she come out? I didn't see her." He looked behind him along the beach, searching for her. "Maybe she's gone to the sand dunes," he said.

"No, Dad."

"I can't see her in the water though. Was she with you?"

"Yes, she was with me a few minutes ago."

Dad came back to me and gripped my arms. His face looked awful. "Is she a good swimmer?" he asked.

"Vaquita can swim like anything. Don't worry about her, she'll be all right." I looked back at the wheelchair high up on the beach and then down at my dad's legs. He didn't even seem to know he was standing. I expected that any moment he was going to realize and then just fall over. I must have been smiling because he shook me a bit.

"Daniel, you're in a daze. Think, boy! Where did you see her?"

I pointed to the place in the water I thought she'd nudged me to, and Dad looked hard and then shook his head. "We've got to do something," he whispered. "You shouldn't have left her."

I knew I was going to have to tell him, but just as I was thinking how to, his hand tightened on my shoulder and there she was. She came suddenly out of the waves. Other people saw her too, and shouted out in amazement. Later, Dad told me she was about forty metres off the shore. She leapt high into the air. Then she twisted round and dived straight back in again, exactly where she'd come out. I saw her properly for the first time. There was a great fin on her back. She had two large flippers and a little pointed face. I saw the funny dark rings around her eyes and her mouth.

"Holy mackerel!" Dad said. "Look! Do you know

what that is?" His voice had gone squeaky. "It's a porpoise, son!"

"Isn't she beautiful, Dad?" I said. "Isn't she just
beautiful?" I felt so happy and so thankful, and so relieved, that I could hardly speak.

"Holy mackerel," Dad said again, "isn't life wonderful, Danny?"

"Yes, and mysterious too," I whispered.

Dad took my hand and squeezed it hard and when
I looked at him, he seemed more like a boy than a
man. His face had gone soft and his eyes were wide.
"Just for a moment," he said, "I had the craziest idea
in the whole world. Don't laugh, Danny, but for a second I thought I was looking at our Mrs Seeping," he
said. Then his face fell. "Where is that woman, Danny,
can you see her anywhere?"

I stared at him with my mouth open. He'd seen her
with his very own eyes, and couldn't let himself know
it! "But Dad, I have to tell you something..."

"No time now, Danny. Where on earth is she?"

Of course, Vaquita didn't come back, and Dad got into
a big panic. He ran up and down the beach calling out
for her and trying to get me to do the same. I looked
at the sea until my eyes hurt. Sometimes I imagined
I really did see her again, but every time it was only
a shadow or a bulge among the waves, and anyway, I

knew she wasn't coming back. The clouds had gone and more people were starting to come onto the beach by then, families with dogs and babies and things.

Dad had been standing on his feet for ages and ages. You wouldn't even have known he'd been in a wheelchair. He kept striding up and down the beach and turning round to see if she'd appeared over the sand dunes. I kept wondering how long it would take her to get to Mexico. I tried to think of her in warm shallow water, thick water as she called it, swimming slowly and rolling over and over and eating squid.

"We've lost her," Dad said finally in a quiet and shaky voice, and he looked very grim. "We'd better get back to the hotel and report it. Are you feeling OK?"

"I'm fine now. I feel good. In fact, I feel great. Do you want to get into your chair now, Dad?" I had my fingers crossed behind my back because I wanted him to say no.

Dad looked down at his feet and then back at the wheelchair. "I'd forgotten all about that thing," he said. "I panicked when I couldn't see you two anywhere. I didn't even think about my legs. Thank God you're all right, my love." He took my face in his hands and gazed at me, and there were tears in his eyes. "Why are you so calm about everything?"

"One of us has got to be calm," I said.

"But Vaquita's gone. This morning she was telling me how much she loved you – 'I love him as if he was mine,' she said, 'he's my sea-friend.' Now she's … vanished."

"Did she say that, Dad? Well, I love her too. She hasn't drowned, I'm sure of it. I know that's what you're thinking." I reached up and wiped my father's face with the palm of my hand. "You've got sand and tears all over you," I told him.

"Come on then, let's go and get some help," he said.

"What about the wheelchair?"

"Leave it for now, Danny. We'll come back for it later."

It was hard for us to walk away from the sea. As we left the beach, Dad kept turning back to stare at the waves. I didn't think I'd ever be able to tell him what it was like under the water with Vaquita. It'd been fantastic and terrifying all at the same time. She'd wanted to take me to the thick waters of Mexico. I don't think she realized at first that I'd have drowned in the water.

When we got back to the hotel, I let Dad do all the talking because I thought it would calm him down. His face was completely white and his hands were shaking all the time. He was sure that Vaquita had drowned. The hotel manager phoned the police and I felt bad because I knew they'd be wasting their time trying to find her. But I could hardly say, "Mrs Vaquita Seeping is a halfling who's become a porpoise again, and she's swum away to Mexico." We had to give them Mr Seeping's address and phone number as well, and Dad and I started worrying about him.

We went back to the place Vaquita and I had left our clothes. Dad sat down on the sand while I got dressed. We both looked at Mum's clothes. "What shall I do with them, Dad?"

"Bury them," he whispered. That was what I was thinking too. I dug a really deep hole in the sand while Dad watched me. Sometimes I stopped and looked back towards the sea. Just as I reached my hand out for Mum's things, Dad stopped me. "One minute, Danny, let me say a proper goodbye." He took Mum's sandals and held them close to his chest for a minute. Then he pulled Mum's dress towards him and buried his face in it. He cried then for a long time without making any noise, and that made me cry too. "Goodbye can take a long time," he said finally, "a very long time," and he handed Mum's clothes back to me and looked away.

After that, we pushed the wheelchair back to the hotel. We both knew we didn't want to be in Treganeth any more. We wanted to go home again and just be quiet.

I packed our things quickly and went into Vaquita's

room. She hadn't slept in her bed at all. Her little suit-case was on the floor, empty. I think she'd just brought it because that's what you do on holiday. Mr Seeping's straw hat was on the bed. I let the water out of the bath and watched it drain away, and I think that's when I said goodbye to her properly. Then I closed the door and went to get Dad.

Chapter Thirteen

Dad fell asleep on our way back home in the coach. I stared out of the window, but I wasn't really looking at anything. I could see things – cars, trees, hills – but they didn't have any meaning to me. I just kept thinking about Vaquita leaping from the water and diving straight back in again in her true body. She had looked so wonderful. Every time I remembered the noise the crowd on the beach made, I couldn't help smiling. There are some boys in school who always call things awesome; I knew what the word really meant now.

Dad woke up halfway through the journey and sat bolt upright.

"What is it?" I asked him.

"We're going to have to face John as soon as we get back." His voice was quivery. "You don't have to come with me; I'll handle it."

"I do have to come with you."

"I think it'd be best if you stay home, love."

"Don't argue with me about it, Dad. We're going together."

Dad bit his lip and stared past me out of the window. "It's not your fault about Vaquita; I want you to know that."

"What's John going to do when we see him, do you think?"

Dad shrugged. "I don't know, I really don't know."

"I've got his straw hat," I said. "Vaquita left it in her room."

"I don't suppose he'll care about that a bit." Dad dropped his head onto his chest and made a groaning noise.

When we got back to Cotton Street, we stopped at the top of the road. Dad was pushing the chair and leaning on it at the same time. I didn't offer to help him, it was the best exercise he'd had since the accident and he didn't even realize.

"We'll go home first," he said. "Then see John when we feel ready."

"I'm coming with you, you know, Dad."

"Yes, of course you are. It's a job we have to do together."

When we were halfway down Cotton Street, Mrs

Malroony came out of her house. "Love you!" she called. I was glad to see her. As strange as she was, she made things feel normal again. "Look at you, Matthew Broadaxe!" she said to my dad. "The sea air must have done you good. Looks like you've got your sea legs."

"I think you're right, Mrs Malroony," Dad said. "How are you?"

"Same as ever. Bored, my dear. Nothing interesting ever happens on Cotton Street. Oh, except shouty man had all the old car tyres moved out of his garden."

I made us some tea when we got in. Neither of us wanted to eat anything. We sat at the kitchen table and Dad kept sighing and reaching over and squeezing my hand. I imagined he was deciding how he was going to talk to Mr Seeping. Then he said, "Look, love. Before we see John, I have to tell you something you don't know yet."

"What, Dad?"

He coughed, and shut his eyes for a moment. "Well, you know how I didn't really want you to get involved with him?"

"Yes."

"This is going to upset you, but it's time you knew. John was the driver of the other car in the accident."

I stood up. "You mean it was all his fault?"

Dad stood up too. "He was driving far too fast on

Cannon Road. Mum and I were coming towards him."
I could hear the clock ticking and Dad's breathing and
my own heart beating. "He came round that sharp
bend at a terrible speed." There was a bird singing
somewhere in our garden; I didn't think it was a wren.
"He was on us before we knew it. I didn't want to tell
you in case you hated him because of it."

"I do hate him!" I shouted.

"No you don't, Danny. Not really." Dad moved towards me and I stepped back out of his way.

"But he killed my mum!"

"This is exactly what I didn't want, you see. John's
suffered horribly because of it. He's never driven a car
since."

"Yes, but he's all right, isn't he!" I knew I was shouting and I couldn't have cared less.

"Calm down, Danny. Is he all right, really? Think
for a minute." I felt tears on my face and I could hear
a roaring sound in my ears. "John's had to live with it
every day, you know."

"Not like us though, Dad!"

"I've forgiven him, and that's what I want you to
try and do."

"Well I never will!" I shouted.

I ran upstairs to my room and banged the door
shut. I fell asleep for a while and when I woke up
again, I was calm. I stared at my face in the mirror.

It was different. It was as if I'd become more solid, more sure.

I could hear Dad moving about on the landing. I wondered what it must have been like for him knowing he'd have to tell me about John one day. I opened the door and he walked in slowly as if he wasn't sure he should. He sat on the edge of my bed and waited for me to speak. "So why didn't you tell me before?" I asked.

"I needed to protect you. You've had far too much to deal with since the accident – looking after me every day, keeping this house in order, and on top of that going to school like any other boy."

"I didn't think you knew what it was like for me. I didn't think anyone could possibly know that."

"I've tried hard to guess what it's been like for you, Danny."

"I've tried to imagine what it's like not being able to walk, but I can't."

"Some days, after you'd gone to school, I'd just sit and weep."

"I sometimes cried at school, Dad, but inside, where nobody could see."

"Was there no one there to talk to?"

I thought about that for a minute. "Do you remember when I burnt your toast and we had a row about me feeding Mr Seeping's fish?" Dad nodded. "I nearly talked to Mr Lovemore that day. He was collecting water-snail eggs for his pond, and I was really miserable. I didn't tell him anything in the end because it was too hard."

"It felt as if nothing would ever change, didn't it, love?"

"Yes, but when I found Vaquita," I said, "everything started to change." Then I realized something – Dad and I had to live without Mum because of what John had done, and now he had to live without Vaquita because we'd taken her away and lost her in the sea.

"And then the miracle happened," Dad whispered, looking down at his legs. "I don't know how, but it did."

As soon as we got to the gate at number seven, I could see something was wrong, but I couldn't tell what it was at first. Then I noticed that the curtains at the front-room window were open, and the front door was wide open as well.

"You don't *have* to see John. If you're feeling angry with him, you can go back home, and I'll talk to him," Dad said.

"I do want to see him. I'm all right. I want to give him his hat back."

We walked down the old cracked path to the door and stopped. "John!" Dad called.

He didn't answer. "He can't be out, Dad. He'd never leave his door open. Do you think something's happened?"

Dad shook his head. "Mrs Malroony would've said something."

Then we did hear a noise inside the house, and we walked in. John was in the fish room, sitting in the middle of the floor. I could hear the sound of seagulls and waves, and the patterns of light on the walls and ceiling flowed slowly into each other and then came apart again.

I heard Dad make a little sound; I'm sure he was amazed by the room. "John," he said, "we've come to say…"

"You don't have to say anything," John whispered. His voice was very hollow sounding and croaky.

"There was nothing we could do," Dad told him. "We waited for ages on the beach, but she never came back."

"It's all right; I knew."

"We reported it as soon as we could."

"I'm not blaming you," John said. He looked as if he'd been crying for a long time. I suspected that the minute we walked away from number seven with Vaquita, he'd begun to weep for her. "I'm not blaming you," he said again. "It was inevitable."

"Maybe she went out too far and there was a

current," Dad said helplessly. "The waves were big as well."

John looked up at us. "She'd have liked that."

"She did like it," I said.

"You're standing, Matt," John whispered.

"I could, suddenly. I saw Danny in trouble in the water, and that was enough."

"It's a gift," John murmured. I knew what he meant, but Dad didn't.

"It's a gift all right, but let's not talk about me."

"Vaquita was very beautiful in the water, Mr Seeping," I said gently. "We went under together."

"And you got to see her how she really is, Danny?"

I nodded. "She rolled and leapt and swam."

"She said you had faraway sea eyes. She thought you were a sea child, Danny. Did you know that?"

"I think so – at the end. I worked it out." I turned Mr Seeping's straw hat round and round in my hands.

"I used to tell her you were a human boy, but she never would believe me."

"She was awesome, Mr Seeping. She came right out of the water once."

"You never told me she came out of the water, Danny," Dad said. "I thought she might have. I thought she was at the sand dunes."

"I tried to tell you, Dad, but you couldn't hear me."

"I was too worried to think straight."

Mr Seeping made a long sigh – the longest and deepest sigh I've ever heard a person make. It was like the sound of a wave as it draws away from the beach again. "Well, she's where she should be now," he said. "Isn't she, Danny?"

I put his hat on the little table. "Yes, and I think she's happy. Come home, Dad."

When we were outside, Dad squeezed my hand. "You were very kind to him. I was afraid you'd be angry. I was afraid you wouldn't be able to forgive him."

"I feel sorry for him. I only felt angry for a while. We lost Mum and he lost Vaquita."

By the time Dad handed the wheelchair back to the council, lots of things about our life had changed. We were making a big kite together with a really long tail and we were looking forward to trying it out. Dad didn't care in the least if the house was untidy. I was so used to tidying up everything that I kept on doing it, and he said things like, "Stop fussing, Danny, can't you? Just leave everything as it is, there are much more important things to do than that."

"You like the magazine edges straight, though."

"That was just frustration, love. It really doesn't matter." He came over and spread the magazines across the table any old how, and it made me laugh.

Then he threw a couple of cushions on the floor and said, "Best place for them."

I still cooked for us sometimes, but he was taking cookery classes and making delicious food at home. He never let me wash up afterwards because he said it spoilt the meal. "Leave it until the morning," he said. "We're not expecting a visit from the Queen, are we?"

"Do you *honestly* not care that the kitchen's in a mess, Dad?"

"When you're busy with other things, Danny, you can't be tidy all the time as well," he told me. As if I didn't know!

Mrs Martin still came to our house from time to time. She'd become so used to bringing us food that I don't think she knew how to stop. "It's like a miracle," she said to Dad, watching him moving around our kitchen.

"Oh, I still get tired, Mrs Martin," he said.

"Don't we all, though? I know I do. But look at you, Mr Broadaxe! People always used to say sea bathing did you good. I was frightened of the ocean when I was a girl," she went on. "I used to imagine monsters lived under the water."

"What kind of monsters, Mrs Martin?" I asked her.

"Oh, you know, Danny. The kind you see in very old maps of the world. Medieval maps with drawings of strange beasties and mermaids and things."

174

Dad and I laughed.

"I don't expect we *do* know about everything that lives under the sea," I said.

Mrs Martin smiled at us. "It's good to see you two laughing, it warms my heart. There've been a few changes around here lately. You know the chap who always used to shout? He's sorting his garden out and he's planning to make himself a pond."

"What's he going to keep in it, Mrs Martin, do you know?"

"Goldfish, he says, big fancy ones."

"Maybe we could have a pond, Danny," Dad said, "and keep fish as well."

I shook my head. "I think it's better for fish to swim freely, not cooped up in someone's pond and going round and round for ever."

Mrs Martin chuckled. "You certainly know your own mind, young man," she said. "Oh, and John Seeping told me he was moving away from Cotton Street. Maybe a nice family will buy the house and do it up a bit."

Neither Dad nor I had known that. Since we'd come home, we'd been to see him a couple of times, but he hadn't told us he was leaving.

"Do you know where he's going, Mrs Martin?"

"He said he was thinking of going to live in Mexico, if you please. I thought that was daft, but I didn't say so, of course. Mind you, he has been in that house by himself for ages now. He said he'd been stuck with one idea for a long time and he hadn't been able to move on and do other things. I didn't know what he was talking about, but he's a nice enough man, isn't he, when all is said and done?"

"Danny and I think so," Dad said, "don't we?"

"When all is said and done, we do," I answered.